On the Banks
of the Bayou

On the Banks of the Bayou

Roger Lea MacBride

Illustrated by Dan Andreasen

HarperCollins*Publishers*

To Paula and Leighton Morrison,
who have retained the joy and wonder of childhood,
and who, like Laura, have never been able to
keep it to themselves

HarperCollins®, ♣®, Little House®, and The Rose Years™
are trademarks of HarperCollins Publishers Inc.

On the Banks of the Bayou
Text copyright © 1998 by the Estate of Roger Lea MacBride
Illustrations copyright © 1998 by Dan Andreasen

Library of Congress Cataloging-in-Publication Data
MacBride, Roger Lea, 1929–1995.
    On the banks of the bayou / Roger Lea MacBride ; illustrated by
Dan Andreasen.
        p.   cm.
    Summary: When Rose moves to Louisiana to live with her aunt Eliza
Jane to finish high school, she is exposed to new cultures, politics, and
ways of life.
    ISBN 0-06-024973-0
    ISBN 0-06-440582-6 (pbk.)
    1. Lane, Rose Wilder, 1886–1968—Juvenile fiction.   [1. Lane, Rose
Wilder, 1886–1968—Fiction.   2. Louisiana—Fiction.]   I. Andreasen,
Dan, ill.   II. Title.
PZ7.M12255On   1998   98-5573
[Fic]—dc21   CIP
                                                                              AC

1 2 3 4 5 6 7 8 9 10
❖
First Edition

Dear Reader:

The book you hold in your hands is the work of my father, Roger Lea MacBride. It continues the childhood story of Rose Wilder Lane, and her mother and father, Laura Ingalls and Almanzo Wilder. Rose treated my father much as she would have treated a grandson and told him many stories about what it was like growing up in Missouri almost a hundred years ago. Dad took those stories and spun them into a series of books based on the facts of Rose's life. On the Banks of the Bayou *is the seventh of those books.*

I'm sorry to have to tell you that my father has passed away. But my sadness is softened some because his work, the stories of Rose's early life, will continue. He left four partially completed manuscripts that continue Rose's tale, right up to the time she is seventeen years old and ready to leave home to start a life of her own.

There will be one more book after this. With the help of the editors at HarperCollins, we will be able to complete the story of Rose and her family as they come into the modern age of the telephone and automobile.

I am very pleased that these stories will be available to new generations of readers. You will find, as I did, that in a hundred years the things young people think and worry about haven't changed all that much.

Abigail MacBride Allen

Contents

Leaving Home

Rose gripped the edge of her chair seat to steady herself. The train had only just begun chuffing away from the depot, so there wasn't any rocking of the car to make her dizzy. It was only her mind spinning.

Moments before, she had left behind the life she'd known as long as she could remember. She'd just had her last glimpse of her short plump mother, standing on the brick platform below the train window.

Mama's gentle face had craned up from under her hat. Her cheeks had shone with tears in the morning light. Her shimmering eyes had searched the windows to blow one more kiss. Her hand had held up her handkerchief, ready for one last wave.

Rose fought back a fresh wave of tears. A painful lump lodged in her throat. The pitifully yearning look on Mama's face broke her heart. Rose hadn't gotten to the window fast enough for Mama to see her one last time. Mama had looked for her, but Rose wasn't there.

Rose turned her face to the dust-streaked window and held her own handkerchief tight against her eyes. She was sixteen years old, a young lady and too old to be carrying on in public. A silent sob wracked her body so hard that she could feel the eyelets on her corset jabbing into her back.

She managed a few deep breaths, mopped her face, and slumped down in the plush chair seat, hoping no one had noticed her.

After two months of waiting for this day to come, suddenly nothing made sense. She fought a strong urge to run down the aisle and jump off the train before it got to moving too fast. She caught a final glimpse of the back-yard of her house as the train pulled away from town. There was poor old Fido, asleep on his favorite patch of cool earth under the oak tree. A pair of Papa's overalls hung dry-ing on the clothesline. The place looked so forlorn and lonely from the train. And then it was gone, and the telegraph poles whizzed past her window faster and faster.

Oh, how could she leave Mama and Papa alone like that, with boarders to feed and keep house for? How could she leave them to run the farm? Who would fetch the water? Who would milk the cow? Who would bring in the stove wood?

She had pestered Mama and Papa every day of the last two months, badgering them with questions and doubts.

"If you miss the work while you're away, we'll be pleased to hold it all for you until you get back," Papa had joked.

"Don't you worry about any of it," Mama had said. "It is only 'til next summer. Why, you'll be back home before you know it. We'll manage."

But these were the very first moments of the biggest adventure of Rose's life. Nine months stretched before her as vast as the sea. She must cross it alone, without Mama and Papa, far from all things familiar. The thought both terrified and exhilarated her.

The train lurched and picked up more speed. The car began to rock. Rose blinked away her tears and tidied her dress. It was a simple dark-blue figured gingham with a lace collar and cuffs. Rose had complained, and begged to wear her favorite white lawn, but Mama insisted she wear the blue one. Mama had said it was extravagant to wear white on a long train journey: "It soils so easily. Blue is more practical. It'll stay looking fresh 'til you get there."

Rose wrinkled her nose against the sharp smell of coal smoke drifting back from the locomotive. Maybe Mama was right, she thought, as she watched the gray tail of smoke writhing away across the fields. Through the soles of her new shoes she felt the rhythm of the wheels clattering over the rail joints.

For nine years—ever since her family had moved to Mansfield, Missouri, from De Smet, South Dakota—she had heard that sound. She heard it no matter where she was, or what she was doing. Many trains passed through Mansfield, and she could even tell from the sound when a train was an express and when it was a local.

The railroad had a language of its own: the clattering of wheels, the whistles, the thunder of steam escaping when the locomotive had stopped at the depot in town.

These sounds came to Rose at her desk at school while she listened to the droning of the teacher; in the henhouse as she fed the chickens their mash; in her bed at night as she drifted off to sleep. The steady drumming of the wheels against the rail joints was the heartbeat of her daily life.

For nine years the mournful whistle had called to her. Sometimes she imagined she was the only one to have heard it. She would often stop in the middle of hoeing the garden to listen to it echo through the hollows of the Ozark Mountains. The trains had sparked Rose's dreams about the great world beyond, the world the trains came from, and the places to which they rushed. The whistle beckoned to her, telling of bustling cities, of buildings tall enough to touch the clouds, of streets filled with laughter and parades and sophistications Rose could only imagine.

Now, finally, her day had come. She didn't have to wonder who was on the trains, and where they were going. She was one of those passengers herself. And she knew where she was going.

The sudden shriek of the locomotive's whistle made Rose flinch.

"Your first time on a train?" The conductor was smiling down at her from under his blue cap. He held her carpetbag in his hand.

"Oh!" Rose cried out. "I forgot!" In the confusion of departing, she had set her bag down on the vestibule floor and left it there.

"Not to worry, young lady." His old eyes

crinkled kindly. "That's what we're here for, to look after our passengers. Your father gave me strict instructions to take care for his little girl. Should I put the bag up on the rack?"

"Yes, thank you," Rose answered. She hated to be called a little girl, but she was grateful.

"Now if you need a thing, all you do is ask." His ruddy cheeks bulged with a smile. "You'll be mine 'til we get to Memphis this evening."

Then he weaved his way down the aisle of the jostling car, from seat to seat, until he got to the end. He opened a door, and a gust of smoke billowed out. Rose could see a man sitting in a parlor chair, smoking a cigar and reading a newspaper. The door closed. Then she noticed a brass sign that read SMOKING ROOM. Only men could sit in there.

Rose looked about her. The car was as cozy as she had expected, although it could use a dusting and it smelled of smoke. The chair seats were covered in red plush, with dark spots at the headrests where there ought to have been antimacassars. The dark wood walls were varnished to a high shine, with clever scrollwork over each window. Coal-oil lamps in pretty brass chandeliers swung from the ceiling.

About a dozen people sat scattered around the car. A woman in a pink-flowered lawn and a broad, feathered hat sat directly across the aisle from Rose. She met Rose's eyes and smiled.

Rose smiled back and then stared shyly into her lap. She was not accustomed to talking to strangers, and she knew her face must still be red and blotchy from crying.

The woman stood up and came across to Rose's chair. "Are you all right, dear?" she said. Her voice had a soothing sound, drawn-out and syrupy. It reminded Rose of a girl she'd once known in school.

"Yes," said Rose.

The next thing Rose knew, the woman had plunked herself down right next to her. Rose caught the scent of lavender. She didn't know what to do or say.

"You mustn't let yourself get too low," the

woman said in a matter-of-fact way. "I left home when I was about your age, myself. It's hard to see it now, but your folks will manage just fine without you."

Rose's head snapped up in surprise. She searched the woman's face. "How did you know?"

The woman laughed gently, and touched Rose's knee. "Your dress is lovely. Your mother is clearly a fine seamstress. Did she make up the lace as well?"

"Yes, she did," said Rose. "Well, Mama tatted the collar and I did the cuffs." She patted down a curled corner of one of her cuffs. She had been in such a hurry, she had made some of the knots too tight.

The train was up to full speed now, and the car banged hard as it rounded a curve. Rose grabbed the back of the chair in front of her for support. Her heart pounded as quickly as the clattering of the wheels. She couldn't help thinking of Paul Cooley's father, who had been killed in a horrible train wreck. The train was going so fast; surely it would fly off the tracks any second.

"My name is Mrs. Harris," the woman said, extending her gloved right hand. "Mrs. Prue Harris."

"Rose Wilder," answered Rose. She reached out with her own gloved hand. In the instant their hands met and shook, Rose felt terribly elegant and sophisticated. A thrill ran along all her nerves. Then she remembered to add, "Pleased to make your acquaintance."

"You are leaving home, and I am returning," Mrs. Harris said, hooking the handle of her parasol over the back of the chair in front of her. "I was born and raised in Arkansas. When I married Mr. Harris, we emigrated out west, to Oregon. We keep a mercantile trade, in Medford. I'm coming back for a visit. My father has died, and I'm coming back to stay a piece with Ma."

"I'm so sorry," Rose said. "It must be terribly sad."

Mrs. Harris nodded gravely, then smiled again. "And where are you bound? On some great adventure, I hope."

Rose decided she liked Mrs. Harris. She was glad to have someone to talk with, even though Mama had warned her again and again not to talk to any strangers. Everyone had told her not to do something while she was away: Don't hold hands with any man out of plain sight; never let your ankles show; don't wear red; don't accept any gift from a stranger; don't do anything to stain your reputation. Lately it had seemed that Rose's life was about all the things she shouldn't do.

Now it felt wickedly good to disobey Mama, and there was no way she would ever know. Something that had been tangled up inside of Rose for a long time was unraveling.

Rose poured out her story. She explained about her aunt Eliza Jane, Papa's sister, who lived in Crowley, Louisiana. Eliza Jane—E.J.—had invited Rose to come and live with her while Rose attended high school. There was no high school in Mansfield.

"I believe it is terribly important for a young woman to have her education," Rose declared. "My aunt E.J. says the times are

changing and women ought to improve themselves for the day when we can have a say in
the affairs of the world."

Mrs. Harris chuckled. "I should say the
times are changing. But I wonder if men will
change with them."

"Oh, I think so," answered Rose. "Paul—
I mean Paul Cooley—he is a dear friend I
grew up with—Paul thinks women should
have the vote. He is very progressive in his
thinking. He is my dearest friend. Why, we
have known each other almost our whole
lives."

Rose rushed on like a logjammed river
suddenly broken loose. Mrs. Harris listened
patiently, offering a small comment or a
chuckle now and again. Rose felt almost as
though she had known Mrs. Harris all her
life, that she could tell her just anything, even something that wasn't quite the
truth.

"Paul and I, we . . . we plan to marry," Rose
said, surprising herself with her own bold-
ness. A wave of heat crept up her neck; then

she added, "After I've finished high school, of course."

Paul Cooley *was* Rose's dearest, oldest friend. He was three years older than Rose, and had been working as a telegraph operator. He had been assigned to Sacramento, California, the state capital and a very important depot. He was trying to save the money to buy a house and some land back in Mansfield.

Paul's mother and father had been best of friends with Rose's mama and papa. The two families had emigrated to Missouri together in covered wagons, nine years ago. After Paul's father died in a train wreck, Paul had had to take care for his mother.

Ever since then Rose thought no boy could be as good or as kind as Paul. And he was handsome to boot. He had a wide, clear forehead, dark sober eyes, and thick hair as dark and shimmery as crow feathers. Sometimes a lock of it fell across his forehead, and when he flipped it back, Rose's heart would melt. Rose loved him, and she knew he loved her back.

He had told Rose that she ought to learn telegraphy, and one day they could work and live in the same town, maybe in Mansfield.

But Paul and Rose had not made plans to marry. In their letters they had written each other about everything else. Yet Rose could read between Paul's lines. She knew they were thinking the same thing, that it would be wonderful to be husband and wife, to be a family instead of just friends.

Riding on the train had unlocked something in Rose. It was as if she had stepped onto a magic carpet and was soaring above the earth, free as a bird, flying away from all her everyday cares and chores. Her dreams were taking flight as well.

Endless Night

Mrs. Harris sat with Rose all the way to Memphis. At noon they ate their dinner together, over handkerchiefs spread on their laps. Mrs. Harris had a box dinner of biscuits with ham that had been made up for her at the Colonial Hotel in Springfield, where she had stayed the night before. She had been traveling for some days now.

Rose had the same molasses tin she'd carried with her to school when she was little. Mama had packed her two thick chicken sandwiches, three carrots, and a hunk of gingerbread. For her supper Mama had put in biscuits with cracklings, and a little crock of molasses to dip them in. Rose would arrive in Crowley in time for breakfast the next morning.

The day grew stifling hot. The stale air in the car was smothering. Rose wanted to open the window, but Mrs. Harris said they dared not because all the dust and clinkers from the locomotive would fly in. So they cooled themselves as best they could with paper fans the conductor gave them. The fans had an advertisement on them for the Frisco System, the railroad they were riding on. It was a picture of a speeding locomotive, with mountains in the background: "East to West, Safest and the Best!"

When Rose grew thirsty, Mrs. Harris showed her the water tank at the end of the car. It had a spigot on it and next to it a metal tube filled with paper cones. Mrs. Harris showed her how to pull one out. The cone was made of waxy paper, glued together so it could hold water without leaking a single drop.

"It's the new sanitary way of drinking," Mrs. Harris said. "You use it and throw it away. It keeps from passing sickness from one person to another." Rose had grown up drinking her water at school from a ladle, dipped into a bucket. Everyone drank from the same ladle. When one scholar came down with the grippe, they all did.

When they weren't chatting, Rose stared out the window, watching the countryside fly past. In small towns she enjoyed watching the strips of earth between the green garden rows flash open and shut as the train roared by. Posters on fences, announcing circuses and Wild West shows, were blurs of bright color. Children in backyards waved, and horses pulling wagons that waited at the grade crossings tossed their heads in terror.

Every so often the express would rocket past a local or a freight train that had been shunted onto a siding. The sudden slamming of air against the window was like an explosion, rattling the frames and setting Rose's heart to pounding. The same thing happened when the train plunged into a dark tunnel. She didn't like the lost feeling of sitting in pitch black racing through space at such a terrifying speed.

As the train crossed the open countryside, the views stretched for miles across the sleepy wooded hills, bathed in the soft blue haze of late summer. Vultures floated in lazy circles above the bald hilltops, and in the wooded hollows where the streams ran, startled blue herons flapped their long wings a few times and then glided away into the trees.

Here and there small shabby farms dotted the landscape: a battered barn, a corn patch, chickens scattered about the barnyard, and a drooping mule hiding from the hot sun in the shade of a tree.

With each sight and each mile, Rose felt herself hurtling far away from home, into a world so enormous and unknowable she could grasp only a corner of it. Her heart filled to bursting with a love for life, for all the lives on earth. How she would like to live every one of them, to see everything the earth had to offer!

The first depot stop was Mountain Grove. Excitement began to ripple through the train even before it had stopped. The conductor called out the name, and a few people began to gather up their belongings and hurry down the aisle to wait by the door. The open land gave way to small shacks, then larger, well-kept homes. Then there was a siding and some warehouses and boxcars being unloaded.

When the train finally slid into the depot, with a great crashing and the roar of escaping steam, Rose saw that a large crowd of people was milling about the platform. Wagons were parked every which way in the street. Every face had an anxious look. Freight wagons were quickly rolled down the platform. Rose watched a young man hug and kiss a young lady good-bye. She was crying. A clutch of boys dashed past.

It was all over in an instant. The conductor cried out, "All aboard!" The car lurched forward, and Mountain Grove faded away behind them.

The Ozark hills rolled on and on. Towns were more spread apart, and the land looked wilder, with deeper hollows and vistas of unbroken forest. Here and there lumber companies had cleared whole ridges of trees.

Before long they had crossed the border into Arkansas at Mammoth Spring, and then the names of the depots flashing past were foreign to Rose: Ravenden, Imboden, Hoxie, Hatchie Coon, Marked Tree. Each one piqued her curiosity: how did that town gets its name, and what was it like to live there?

After some hours the hills smoothed out and the land became level as a tabletop, with trees only along the hedgerows, checkerboarded with fields of tall corn, and scraggly cotton. She began to see more and more black people, although not one came to sit in the car she was riding in. She knew from visiting the depot in Mansfield, and from her reading, that everywhere in the south of the country there were Jim Crow laws.

Jim Crow was the name of an old minstrel song that made fun of black people. Jim Crow laws said blacks must be kept separate from white people.

Rose knew that black people were never treated as well as white people. In the South in recent years a hundred black men had been hanged by lynch mobs in the dark of night, without a shred of justice.

At the Mansfield depot, there were separate waiting rooms. The waiting room for whites was clean and well lit, and it had a large heater stove in it for the winter. The waiting room for blacks was always untidy, cold, and dark.

Because of the Jim Crow laws, blacks could not get a haircut in the same barbershop as whites, use the same doorway to a hotel, or ride in the same train car.

Rose had seen only a few black people before, and had never met one. But she knew it was hateful the way America had treated them. She felt as if she were going to a foreign country, knowing she would be living where a black person could be lynched and no one could do a thing to stop it. How could a country that said it believed all folks were created equal treat some of them so shabbily?

Just when Rose had grown weary of the flatness of the landscape, Mrs. Harris pointed at something outside the window and chirped, "Look, there it is!"

Rose looked, but she couldn't see anything.

"There, between those clumps of trees. It's the Mississippi!"

Rose spied a glitter of water. But it wasn't until the car first clattered onto the long bridge that she saw the magnificence of it. Rose had never seen a river so wide. No wonder the Indians called it the Father of Waters.

It made Rose's legs tingle to look down and realize that just the thin rails and the spider-like trestle kept them from falling into the muddy, rushing water. She almost couldn't look out the window after that.

As soon as the train left the bridge, it passed enormous brick factories spewing smoke and foul odors from brick chimneys that were taller than any tree could ever grow. The streets swarmed with wagons and buggies, and Rose even caught her first glimpse of a locomobile. She laughed aloud at the sight of it, a buggy moving by itself without a horse.

The train began to slow as it passed through a neighborhood of gray shacks where she could see only blacks. She saw older people sitting on their porches while children played in the dusty streets.

Then she began to see larger well-kept houses and barns, beautiful lawns and shrubbery, then stores and shops that were fancier than anything she had seen before. She saw streets paved with bricks and was amazed to see a streetcar heading down one of those streets, straight toward the train. Rose thought for certain the streetcar would collide with the train. The motorman was clanging the bell as he brought the heavy steel car to a sudden stop, a few feet from the grade crossing.

The train crept into a huge iron barn, big as a mountain, with a domed roof covered with hundreds of panels of glass. The rush of steam from the locomotive boomed and echoed hollowly. Bells clanged and brakes screeched.

Throngs of people cluttered the platforms. Every kind of person was there, from farmers in their battered overalls to men and women in the kind of finery Rose had only seen in magazines such as *The Woman's Home Companion.*

Black men in red uniforms and caps rushed about like bees, loading and unloading rows of freight wagons piled with packages and trunks and crates. Other trains stopped on other tracks emitted plumes of smoke and steam that rose to the roof. Shafts of light pierced the hazy air, cutting golden columns. All that activity made a steady roar in Rose's ears, like a rushing river.

This was Memphis, one of the great cities of the South.

Mrs. Harris helped Rose with her grip, and they followed the crowd of shuffling passengers off the train. Both of them would make connections with other trains. Standing on the platform, saying good-bye to Mrs. Harris, Rose felt her pulse flutter with excitement. She realized suddenly that she was about to be on her own again. Her self-confidence deserted her when the scuffling, jostling crowd swallowed up Mrs. Harris.

The clamor of locomotives and voices calling out and carts rattling past made her light-headed. A man with a large, red nose, wearing a derby and carrying a little dog, eyed her intently. Rose shrank back toward the steps of the car, bumping into the conductor.

"There you are!" he said heartily. "Thought I'd lost you. Now you just follow me. Give me your grip. The train to Baton Rouge is on track four. You have only twenty minutes to catch it."

Rose followed the conductor as best she could, into the surging crowd. Her eyes bulged with the sights and sounds of a great city depot. She had never been among so many people before, all in so great a hurry that many bumped into her without so much as a grunt of apology.

She followed the conductor up a wrought-iron stairway, then across a bridge right over the train. She could see all the trains lined up, and feel the vast space under the roof. Pigeons fluttered back and forth in the rafters. She followed the conductor back down another set of stairs, and up to a train car. Then the conductor was speaking to another conductor, handing him Rose's ticket and grip, and he was gone.

The new conductor helped Rose up the stairs, put her grip on the luggage rack, and left her to get settled again. Rose couldn't see much from this train, but she was glad not to be fighting her way through the people on the platforms. She wondered how anyone could live in such a noisy, crowded place.

She ate her supper alone as the train clattered south through Mississippi. Again the car was nearly empty, and not very tidy. Orange rinds, scraps of paper, and a squashed cigar littered the floor.

As the sun lowered in the sky, a news butch came through.

"Fresh salted peanuts a dime, ten cents! Salted peanuts for one thin dime!" he cried out in a raspy voice.

He couldn't have been even as old as Rose, but he needed a shave and his jacket was threadbare at the collar and cuffs. Newspapers and magazines stuck out of a soiled bag slung over his shoulder, and he had a stack of boxes of peanuts in his hands.

"Are they fresh?" a woman down the aisle asked.

"Yes, ma'am, they sure are," he shot back. "Yes, ma'am! I just got done dusting 'em off." Then he laughed hoarsely at his own joke.

The woman grimaced. "Well, if they are as fresh as you, you can keep them."

As he passed Rose he reached out to give a box to her, and winked. Without thinking, she took it. Just as quickly she called out, "No! I mean, I'm sorry. Thank you very much."

"All you can eat for a dime," he pleaded, wiping his nose on his sleeve. "Help a poor fellow out."

"No," Rose said, blushing. She hated to

draw attention to herself. She set the box down on the armrest and turned to stare out the window. She could feel the butch watching her, and then he muttered something and shuffled off down the aisle and into the next coach. She was relieved to see the box was gone.

He came back through later, this time selling strawberry soda pop. Rose kept her face turned to the window, and he didn't bother her again.

The flat countryside no longer held her interest, so she tried to read a newspaper someone had left behind. But there was nothing in it she cared about. As the last light left the land, she drifted off into a fitful sleep.

She awoke now and again, when the train pulled into depots along the Mississippi, at towns whose names she knew well from studying the War Between the States: Vicksburg and Natchez.

On and on into the night the train raced, farther and farther south. Rose didn't like riding through the darkness, with the lanterns turned so low she could barely read her watch. There was nothing to see and nothing to do. The night stretched endlessly before her.

She could have rented a pillow from the conductor for twenty-five cents, but she didn't want to squander her money. She had five dollars, more money than she had ever carried. It was from Mama's egg money and only for an emergency. Rose had promised herself she wouldn't waste a penny.

So she tried to sleep sitting up, trying to stay neat, feeling more and more exhausted and untidy and uncomfortable. How could she be tired when all she'd done all day was sit?

In the middle of the night, the train reached Baton Rouge. Rose changed trains again. This time she had to wait almost two hours in the nearly empty depot. For a long time she just sat on a bench in the waiting hall. A man was lying on a bench asleep, snoring. A woman sat stone-faced with her little girl asleep in her lap.

Outside Rose could hear the grinding and

clattering of freight trains shunting back and forth in the yards. She got up and looked at the brightly colored posters advertising special excursion trains to this place and that.

Finally she mustered the courage to go to the ladies' waiting room. She washed her face for the first time in a porcelain sink with indoor plumbing. The roller towel was so dirty she didn't want to use it, so she dried herself with her handkerchief.

She wondered how the water got pushed through the pipes without someone pumping it. There was a closet, too, with an indoor commode. A sign on the wall read: PULL CHAIN. Rose thought she'd never want to live in a house that had an indoor commode. It'd be like living in a henhouse.

She caught her last connection at four o'clock in the morning, just as the first birds had begun to twitter outside in the trees. With the graying of dawn, her spirits lifted, and she felt her energy flowing back.

She strained to see what she could as the train clattered across another great bridge.

She was recrossing the Mississippi, heading west. Then the train rumbled onto another trestle, this one endless. For miles and miles the only thing to see was swamp, with dense tangled undergrowth and enormous trees growing right out of the water.

For the first time, Rose saw clumps of Spanish moss, hanging like tatters of morning fog that had gotten snagged on the branches. It was just as she had seen it in pictures, a murky, forbidding landscape, a scene from a disturbing dream.

The sun rose as the train reached Lafayette. Rose felt a tingle of excitement running all through her. She tapped her foot impatiently as the train puffed and stuttered out of each town. The conductor had told her in Lafayette, "Four more stops, miss." She counted them and recounted them.

Then, finally, the conductor called out, "Crowley is next! Crowley in two minutes!"

Rose was standing at the door, her grip in her hand, before the train had even begun to slow.

A New Home

"Yoo-hoo! Rose, dear!"

Eliza Jane Thayer, Rose's aunt, came rushing toward her through the hubbub on the depot platform like a charging bull. The peacock feather in her hat quivered, and her face beamed. Her little boy, Wilder, dressed in a Buster Brown suit, his hair plastered down wet and cheeks still pink from a fresh scrubbing, had to skip to keep up.

"There you are." E.J.'s voice rang out like church bells. Rose couldn't help laughing. She was giddy from sleeplessness and excitement, and she found E.J.'s high spirits catching.

A New Home

"I just can't say how worried I've been, ever since I got your mother's wire saying you'd left. A young girl traveling all that way by herself!" E.J. brushed a stray thread from Rose's shoulder, then took Rose by the arm. She sized Rose up with her dancing eyes.

"But here you are, looking as fine as . . . Are you all right? Of course, you must be tired. And famished, I'm sure. Well, Viola has cooked up a hearty breakfast, just on your account. Wilder, fetch your cousin's grip, now.

"Come along, Rose darling. I've so much to tell you. Your trunk arrived last week. I had it put up in your room, and . . ."

Rose floated alongside E.J. as if in a vivid dream. She was woolly-headed, yet, at the same time, she felt oddly alert and awake. The crowd on the platform, the brick depot, the train, even the clouds in the pale-blue sky all looked especially bright and cheerful, crisp as a stereograph.

They made the short trip to E.J.'s house in a hired hack driven by a man in overalls and a tall planter's hat. "À la maison, Claude," E.J.

said to him when they settled in their seats.

"Oui, madame," he replied, and the hack jerked forward, away from the depot. E.J. and Wilder sat next to each other on the seat opposite Rose. E.J.'s eyes sparkled with pleasure. Wilder stared at Rose with a shy smile on his face. For a moment, no one spoke. Then they all started talking at once.

"Oh, I do so envy you, Rose!" E.J. exclaimed, when they had stopped laughing. She popped open her parasol. It was early, but the sun already felt hot on Rose's shoulders, and the air was sticky.

Rose chuckled. "Whatever for?"

"I remember when I first came to this region, how impressed I was by it all: the French, the Negroes, the strange customs, and the mysterious beauty of the bayous. I just know you'll find it ever so interesting."

E.J. stopped chattering long enough to tell the driver something. "We'll take a little tour, the long way home," she explained. "So you can have a look-see at the heart of our fair city."

E.J. pointed out this and that, called out to some acquaintance on the sidewalk, and scolded Wilder for banging his shoes against the seat. Rose half listened, her eyes filling with first impressions of Crowley.

It was big, she decided right away. From the depot the wagon drove onto an enormous, wide boulevard, Parkerson Avenue, the main street. Parkerson stretched for countless blocks, and it was muddy brown like a broad, slow-moving river. It was wide enough for several wagons to easily pass at the same time, and teemed with traffic.

Large, well-kept buildings lined the street on both sides: mercantile houses of every description, barbershops, offices, a large opera house. The street had been paved in places with wooden blocks, and all along it were new sidewalks, some of them made of concrete. Rose even saw a sign for an ice-cream parlor. Her heart leaped with joy. Crowley was a real city! E.J. had said five thousand souls called it home. That was more than ten times the size of Mansfield.

Every side street, on both sides, was lined with houses. Some of them were cozy-looking cottages with low-pitched roofs. Others were large, two-story houses with outdoor stairways. But all the houses had one thing in common: a beautiful covered porch. Some were fancy, with scrollwork and carved columns. Some porches wrapped around the sides of the houses, and the two-story houses had a second covered porch on the top floor. A porch gave a house such a contented look.

"They are called galleries here," E.J. said. "It's so hot in these parts, and it rains so often, that folks need a dry, shady place to get some air."

"It's very flat here," Rose said. "And there are hardly any trees." She could see saplings and some young trees, but none of the stately old oaks and hickories that she was accustomed to in the Ozarks. Here, where there were no houses, there was not a single tree.

"It's prairie," Wilder piped up. "Prairie and swamp. Indians used to live here 'til the

Spaniards and the French came. I hope you like croquet."

"I do like croquet," Rose said. "Although I have only played it once, and I'm not very good."

"Me neither."

"Either," E.J. corrected. She had been a schoolteacher and wouldn't have her own son speak anything but perfect English. "Or 'Neither can I.'"

"Yeah, either," Wilder said, sighing.

"You have grown so since I last saw you," Rose said. "And it was only last spring you visited in Missouri."

"I'm eight years old now," he crowed.

In the middle of the town, halfway down Parkerson Avenue, was the grandest building Rose had ever laid eyes on. It was the tallest in the whole city, soaring five stories high with beautiful columned porticos all around and dozens of tall glass windows. On top of the building rose a tall round tower with a dome, covered in green tile. On the very top was a statue, which E.J. explained was of blind Justice holding her scales.

"It looks like the palace of a king," Rose exclaimed. She had seen magnificent buildings just like it in pictures of the World's Columbian Exposition in Chicago, which had been held when she was a little girl.

"It is our new courthouse," E.J. said proudly. "And the seat of Acadia Parish. They call a county a parish here, Rose. The courthouse is just finished up, and not even dedicated yet."

Around the courthouse was a lovely park with new plantings of young trees and wrought-iron benches to sit on.

Claude drove the hack all the way around the courthouse, and then halfway around again. Then they headed east on another broad boulevard, Hutchinson Avenue, where there were fewer houses. Then Claude turned the hack right onto a side street.

"We are just a few blocks down, to the left," E.J. announced.

Finally the hack slowed in front of a very large house and turned into the lane.

"Well, here we are," E.J. sang out. Rose gasped. The house was two and a half stories high, with a large wraparound gallery and columns and a whole wraparound gallery on the second floor as well. It looked as tidy and crisp as a freshly made bed and, to Rose's small-town eyes, big as a hotel.

"Oh, E.J. It's . . . it's so grand," was all she could think to say.

"Big, isn't it?" E.J. said grimly. "I couldn't keep up the whole thing myself, what with Mr. Thayer gone to his reward. The second floor is let out to the manager at one of the rice mills. Mr. Thayer had it built just before he died. Thank goodness, too, because his family could have taken it from me, along with the rest of his estate."

Rose was about to ask how Mr. Thayer's family could do that when E.J. waved her hand in disgust.

"But no more of that now. Let's get you freshened up and fed."

Inside, the house was just as lovely as outside. The rooms were spacious and airy, trimmed all around with the most beautiful mahogany moldings. The front rooms and dining room were separated by enormous sliding doors that disappeared into the walls when they weren't needed. Every room had a flowered carpet, and flowered wallpaper. There was a parlor with a beautiful suite all covered in pale-blue silk, with silk tassels on the arms and silk fringe around the bottoms.

E.J. even had a sitting room, with a piano in the corner and a whole library of books in glass-fronted shelves.

Photographs of the family hung on some of the walls. There was one of Papa, E.J., and their brothers and sisters, made when Papa was a boy. Rose could hardly tear her eyes from it. She saw that Wilder's eyes looked like Papa's.

When E.J. showed her her room, Rose could have cried from joy. It was a small room, but it glowed with light and warmth. The curtains were yellow-and-white flowered. They moved softly in the morning breeze coming through the window. The wallpaper was also yellow-flowered.

Rose's trunk was already set up in the corner, with a fresh towel neatly folded on top. E.J. had even laid out Rose's dressing sacque on the bed. A Bible lay on the dresser next to the yellow-striped pitcher and washbasin. And in a small vase was a pink rose.

An ingrain carpet lay on the floor, and an embroidered coverlet lay on the bed. A large pink rose blossom had been sewn in the middle, and there was green sprigging all around the edges.

"A rose for a rose," E.J. quipped, and Rose laughed.

"Oh, E.J., it's just perfect. I had no notion it would be so perfect." She threw her arms around her aunt and gave her a fierce hug. E.J. smelled of strong perfume. "I love you. You're the best aunt a girl could ever have."

E.J. giggled into Rose's ear and stammered, "Oh, well, now. Aren't you the sweetest niece an old aunt could ever want." She gave Rose an extra squeeze and then said, "Now you must meet Viola, and taste her cooking!" E.J. grabbed Rose's hand and led her down the dark hall through a swinging door into the kitchen.

The smell of strong coffee, fresh bread, and sizzling meat set Rose's mouth watering. Then she spotted Viola, setting a bowl of oranges and bananas on the table. Rose tried not to show her surprise, but her tongue froze when Viola called out, "Oh, Miss Wilder! You are even more purty than Mrs. Thayer bragged."

Viola's skin was chestnut brown. Her broad, smiling face and bare arms were damp from the heat of the stove. Her smooth skin shone all over like the finish on a fine piano. She wore a bright-yellow calico dress and a blue-and-yellow bandanna around her head. Her eyes were dark and mirthful and her smile was brighter than any sun.

Rose had never met a black person before she came to Crowley, and now E.J. had a hired girl, and she was black.

Rose blushed hard. "Pleased to meet you," she murmured.

"Sit, dear," ordered E.J. "Now Viola, don't you see you're embarrassing the poor girl? Have you put out the cups yet?"

Rose forced herself not to stare, but she stole every glance she could. Viola was as lively as a canary, busily moving around the kitchen setting down plates and bowls and grabbing a coffeepot off the stove. Rose guessed that Viola might be just a few years older than she.

Viola served the coffee, pouring from a pot in each hand. Thick, steaming black coffee poured out of one pot and thick, steaming milk poured out of the other. She was expert at it, not spilling a single drop on the clean white tablecloth.

"*Café au lait,*" E.J. explained. "It means 'coffee with milk,' in French. Coffee is the great passion of Louisiana folks. It is the French influence. This is the way they drink it."

The coffee was delicious. Rose could almost drink it without sugar, it was so rich.

She ate an enormous breakfast, including a new dish she'd never tasted that Viola called "lost bread." She had dipped slices of stale bread in eggs beaten with cream and sugar, then fried it up. They ate it with cane syrup, which Viola called *"cuite."*

It felt odd to Rose to be served her meal. Since she was old enough to work a knife peeling potatoes, Rose had helped Mama in the kitchen. She had always envied girls she knew whose families had hired help.

But it seemed the most natural thing in the world for E.J. and Wilder. And Viola didn't act like a hired girl. She made jokes with E.J. and carried on like a member of the family. Only she didn't sit down to eat with them.

After breakfast Rose looked around the rest of the house. Wilder had his own little room across the hall from hers. It was neat as a pin, with a little desk where he could do his school studies, and an animal skeleton on his dresser.

E.J.'s room had a large four-poster bed with a round contraption at the ceiling, covered in a kind of gauzy cloth that was bunched up and draped to one side of the bed. She had noticed one in her room as well.

"Those are testers," Viola explained when Rose had returned to the kitchen. Viola stood at the sink, scrubbing the fry pan. Rose noticed for the first time that the sink had a faucet for indoor plumbing. The water came right into the house! Then she noticed an electric lightbulb hanging from the ceiling by a cord.

"May I help?" Rose offered.

"Oh, no, honey. I'm mostly done with the dishes. Aren't there testers in Mizzourah? Don't you have skeetahs?"

"Skeetahs?" Rose wondered. "Oh, mosquitoes! Well, no, we don't have very many. The ground is very rocky there. The water drains away so fast, they haven't a chance to grow."

"Lawd, child. We've got water everywhere," Viola said, laughing. "And we've got skeetahs everywhere, too. They are the most blood-hungriest critters you've ever seen, and make you sick as a dog with malaria. They come out at night. When you go to bed, you best tuck that tester all 'round under the mattress, and then they can't eat you up."

Rose shook her head in amazement. Everything in Louisiana seemed so exotic and unusual. She really was in a foreign country. And so far she loved it.

I Can Do It!

Rose was too keyed up to stay put, so E.J. said Wilder could take her for a walking tour around the city.

"Just be sure to be back for dinner," she said. "You'll want to rest, Rose. Everyone takes a siesta after dinner. And we have an appointment in the afternoon to see Professor Stover at the high school."

Rose's stomach fluttered. She had been studying all summer for the examinations she knew she'd have to take to be enrolled in Crowley High School. She felt ready, and E.J. had said it was as good as certain that she would pass. But Rose still worried. What would happen if E.J. were wrong?

She washed up and changed into a fresh waist and a black skirt that wouldn't show the dust. Except on Parkerson Avenue, there were no sidewalks, and the streets were covered with a thick layer of dirt and leavings. She fussed with her hair, borrowed one of E.J.'s parasols, and out they went.

Across the street from E.J.'s house they walked through a beautiful park with a gazebo where a band could play, and there were smooth lawns for croquet. Then they walked a few blocks to Parkerson Avenue, past many large homes.

Most of the houses were so new that the lawns were mangy-looking. With only a few spindly trees for shade, those places looked forlorn and parched in the harsh light. The air shimmered with waves of heat.

A tank wagon pulled by two slouching mules passed them. A black man in a battered straw hat held the reins. He pushed a lever, and the wagon sprayed a canopy of water on

the street, to keep down the dust. Steam rose
from the dampened earth.

They had only gone a block, and Rose was
already damp with sweat. "My goodness!
How do you stand this heat? I hope it cools off
in winter."

"It's not so hot all the time," Wilder said.
"This isn't so bad anyway. We ought to get
Mother to let us go swimming at the canal! I
just know she would."

"We'll see," said Rose, but she thought it
was too hot even for swimming.

At Parkerson Avenue they turned and
walked toward the courthouse. E.J. had given
Rose two nickels to buy themselves each an
ice cream. They sat in the parlor on wire-
backed chairs at a small wrought-iron table.
A waiter took their order. Wilder ordered a
chocolate soda, and Rose had plain vanilla ice
cream.

Rose had never sat in a restaurant or an
ice-cream parlor. She was nervous, but the
waiter smiled at her, and no one else seemed
to notice how awkward she felt.

They enjoyed the cool sweet taste and the air stirred by an electric fan. Wilder tried to catch flies in his fist, until Rose told him to stop before he knocked something over.

Rose marveled at everything and everyone she saw. It was wonderful to be out among so many people, and to notice how they dressed, and study the sounds of their voices.

Near their table a woman and a young girl spoke to each other in what Rose was certain must be French. Whatever it was, it flowed like music. She just knew that what they were saying was as lovely as the words sounded.

The waiter and some of the other customers spoke with the syrupy, taffy-pulling accent of the South that she had heard so often on the train trip down. It was pretty too, in its own way; friendly and restful. She also heard accents that didn't sound like accents at all, the way E.J. and Wilder spoke. Rose thought she had no accent either.

At the rear of the ice-cream parlor, there was a screened door to the outside. A young black girl wearing a kerchief on her head stood there buying an ice-cream cone from the waiter. She stayed outside in the hot sun and handed her money through the partially opened door. The waiter handed her her cone, and she walked away.

Rose had seen a sign when they walked in: NEGRO CUSTOMERS AROUND BACK. Black people were not allowed to sit in the parlor and enjoy their ice cream with the cooling breeze from the fan on their necks. Rose felt a pang of guilt at her good fortune. The guilt took away some of the pleasure.

As they walked down and around the courthouse and back, Rose tried to think of things to talk about with Wilder. She felt so old and wise with him. It was hard to think like a child. She asked him about school, but only got one-word answers.

"And Uncle Perley, do you see him much?" Perley was Papa's brother. He lived with his wife and baby boy—Rose and Wilder's cousin—in Mermentau, a town close to Crowley. Perley was a rice farmer.

"'Most every Sunday," Wilder said. "Sometimes we go swimming, in Bayou Plaquemine. We saw an alligator there once. It was big, as big as an old log. Uncle Perley said that 'gator was so big, it could eat a whole dog in one bite."

"Really!" Rose breathed. "How gruesome. I do hope I can see one. Were you scared?"

"A little, I reckon."

"What about your father, Wilder? Do you remember him much?"

"Not too much. He was old. Folks say he was rich, too."

"It must be terribly sad not to have a father," Rose said softly. "I have a dear friend, Paul, who lost his father at a young age, in a train wreck. It was terribly sad for him."

Wilder shrugged and kicked at a clod of dirt. "I suppose."

They walked in silence after that. Rose tried to remember how many years it had been since E.J.'s husband, Mr. Thayer, had died. It was only a week or so after Grandfather Wilder died. And in that same year Rose's aunt Laura, Papa and E.J.'s sister, also died. Rose thought it was about four years ago, when Wilder was still a baby.

E.J. had talked her mother and father into coming to Louisiana, and her sister Laura, and Perley, too. But their father—Rose and Wilder's Grandfather Wilder—lost his fortune right after he got there, in a bad business investment. He lost his will to live and died soon after.

So in one year E.J. had lost half the family she had in Crowley, and her poor widowed mother was left unable to keep her own house.

On top of everything else, after Mr. Thayer died, his family took almost all of his money away from E.J. Rose couldn't remember why they could do that, but E.J. had said it was something to do with Mr. Thayer's first wife, who had died, and the strange laws in Louisiana. It had been monstrously unfair.

E.J. had said she was the perfect example for why women should have the vote: "They don't call it suffragism for nothing," she'd groused.

* * *

By the time they got back to the house, Rose was wilted from heat and fatigue. She could barely keep her eyes open at dinner, and it was too hot to eat. She lay down in her bed afterward and fell into a feverish sleep.

E.J. woke her at four o'clock. A hot, dusty breeze blew in the window as Rose washed and dressed in her best lawn. Then she and E.J. rode in a hack to the high school to see Professor Stover.

The school was almost as big as the parish courthouse. And like the courthouse, it was new. Three stories tall and as wide as a city block, it had a large bell tower on top, sculptured dormers in the roof, and a grand entrance with an enormous arch at the top of a wide stairway. Something inside Rose shriveled. She would be lost in such a large place.

Inside it smelled of freshly waxed floors and new paint. Electric lights hung in the hallway. Every room they passed had been scrubbed, the desks lined up and polished, and the blackboards washed perfectly clean in readiness for the scholars. School would start the next week.

Professor Stover's secretary showed E.J. and Rose into the principal's office. It was grand, too, with a high ceiling, shelves and shelves of books, a large globe on a brass stand, many comfortable chairs to sit in, and some tables, too.

Professor Stover stood up from behind a broad, cluttered mahogany desk. He took off his reading glasses and greeted E.J. and Rose with a handshake. He was not as old as Rose thought he might be. He had dark hair, and a smooth face. He smiled at her with his head tilted slightly, like a curious cat. When they all sat down to chat, Rose squirmed under his gaze.

He asked Rose a few questions about her old school in Mansfield, and about the texts they had used there, and how she liked her teachers.

"I didn't like them very well."

"Rose!" E.J. scolded. Then turning to

Professor Stover, she said, "My niece is a very bright girl, I can assure you. She comes from a very small town, somewhat poor-folksy, I'm afraid. Not the sort of town to attract the very best teachers. But her mother, my sister-in-law, was a teacher and gave her lessons at home, and she has studied well on her own."

Professor Stover pulled his chin thoughtfully as E.J. chattered on. Rose felt her dander getting up. She didn't like to be spoken for.

"I have myself taught in small towns, Miss Wilder," Professor Stover finally said. "I know exactly what you feel. I am glad to hear you didn't like your teachers so well. Discontent with the way things are often gives the foundation to a great mind."

Rose allowed herself to gloat for just an instant.

"I take it on faith that you are a good student, and are prepared to make the effort. But . . ." He fished into the piles of paper on his desk, and pulled out one sheet. A locomotive whistle cried out in the silence. Rose nervously picked at a seam in her skirt.

"But I see that you have no official record of having completed your studies through the eighth grade. We would require you to sit for a series of examinations in all our subjects. If you pass them all, we will be happy to admit you."

"Yes sir," Rose answered. "I thought that I would have to take examinations. I have been studying all summer."

"Good, then," Professor Stover said, smiling broadly. He looked back down at the paper in his hand. "Let's see, we will need you to sit for American History, English History, Latin, Algebra, Plane Geometry, Civics, and American Literature."

Rose heard nothing after the word "Latin." She had never studied Latin. She didn't know the first word of Latin. She could never pass an examination in it. Her heart began to sink.

"Is Latin necessary?" she asked in a small voice.

"Oh, yes," said Professor Stover. "It is a requirement to graduate. Latin, of course, is the basis of all the classical studies."

Rose sat thinking what to say.

"You have studied Latin, I assume."

Rose hung her head. "No, it is the only subject I have not studied." Her mind was racing. "Is it so very difficult?"

"Not so difficult. Not as complex as French. But without some basic experience with Latin," the principal said, "I don't see how we could enroll you."

"Oh, dear," E.J. said, wringing her hands. "Oh, dear, Rose. If only I had known, you might have studied it some in Mansfield."

But Rose hadn't come all this way for nothing. She thought hard for a moment, then said, "I think I can learn the Latin you require. How many years is it?"

"Three," the principal said. "But you would be very busy with your other studies. I don't see how—"

"I can do it!" Rose declared. Then she added quickly, "I'm sorry, Professor Stover. I didn't mean to interrupt. But if I pass all my other examinations, would you let me try to do all the Latin in one year?"

Professor Stover sat back in his chair and stroked his chin, gazing at Rose through narrowed eyes. Rose had to control herself from begging. She wouldn't, but every speck of her being wanted to cry out "Please, *please!*"

"What makes you think you can achieve all of that?" he finally said. "This is going to be our first high school graduating class. We want to set a good example for the younger scholars who are coming up. And we want to show the school board that our curriculum is rigorous. Would it be fair to the others if I allowed you to enroll without the same requirements?"

"I don't know if that is fair or not," Rose said. "But if a scholar wants more than anything in the world to graduate from high school, and if she has come all this way to do it, would it be fair to turn her away without giving her the chance to try?"

Rose thought she saw a glimmer of a smile on Professor Stover's lips. He put his fingers together and looked at E.J. "Mrs. Thayer? Anything to add?"

Rose had to gulp for her breath.

"I have been a schoolteacher myself," E.J. said. "I have had students who are highly driven to succeed and can do the work of two or even three ordinary students. I trust that if Rose says she can do it, she will."

"Very well, then," Professor Stover said. "We will let you try, Miss Wilder. But I feel to warn you: It won't be easy. And you must first pass all your other examinations."

"Yes sir," Rose breathed with relief. "Yes sir, I will put all my heart into it. I promise!"

Defeater of Distance

Rose passed all her examinations. She sat in the principal's office for a whole sweltering day. Each examination was an hour long, and she finished each one before the time was up.

She knew plane geometry and algebra because she was purely crazy for them. She hadn't learned arithmetic well, but in Mansfield she had borrowed an algebra text and one on plane geometry from Mrs. Sherwood, the nice old lady who lived across the street.

Even though she had quit school that year

61

out of boredom, as she had every year, she learned to do all the problems by herself. Lying on her stomach in the haymow of the barn in town, she ate apples and solved problems. It was an odd thing for a girl her age, but she just liked doing it.

Luckily, she had read many English novels and much English poetry, so she could answer most of the English history questions. The rest was easy.

Professor Stover told Rose she had done better than he had hoped on her examinations, and he knew she would master Latin.

"We are pleased to enroll you in the class of 1904," he said, shaking her hand. Rose walked all the way back to E.J.'s that afternoon, with a smile that wouldn't leave her face. Not even the awful heat could dull her happiness.

Rose spent the next few days before school took up trying on her new life and learning its rhythms. For the first time, she could sit in the kitchen and read by electric light. It was astonishing how a tiny glass ball hanging from a thread of wire could light the whole kitchen as if it were daytime. She didn't have to huddle close to the little circle of soft light thrown by a coal-oil lamp.

E.J. didn't care to have electricity in the house, but she said Mr. Thayer had insisted on having an electric light in the kitchen.

"It is convenient in the winter, when it's dark at suppertime," she said. "The light makes cooking and washing up so much easier. But electricity scares me."

At quarter to ten at night, the light would blink once, and then at ten o'clock sharp, it would go out. That was when the electric plant shut down. The men at the plant blinked the lights to give everyone time to light their coal-oil lamps. Then all the electric lights in town went dark.

But the telephone was the convenience that most intrigued Rose. It also was in the kitchen, a wooden box on the wall with two bells, a crank, a forked switch to hold the heavy ear receiver, and the mouthpiece sticking out from the middle. It looked like a face with one ear.

The bells rang often during the day, stuttering short and long rings that everyone on the line knew. E.J.'s ring was two longs and one short. When they heard two longs and one short, they were supposed to pick up the receiver and listen to see who was calling. Otherwise, you weren't supposed to answer.

One afternoon when E.J. was in her room napping, Rose and Wilder played checkers at the kitchen table. The phone rang—three shorts.

Wilder jumped up and ran over to the box. He climbed up on a chair, and put his hand over the mouthpiece. Then he stealthily picked up the receiver and put it to his ear.

"Wilder, what are you doing?" Rose demanded. Wilder glared at her and held a finger to his lips. Then he beckoned to her.

"What are you doing?" she asked.

He handed her the receiver and whispered, "Listen!"

Rose held the receiver to her ear. She heard crackling and jerked it away in surprise.

Wilder pushed it back against her ear.

"Mrs. Detweiler?" a woman's irritated voice said, sounding as if she were talking into a jar. "Is that you, Velma?"

"Yes. Who is calling?" another woman's voice answered.

Rose guffawed, then clapped a hand over her mouth. She was overhearing people speak on the telephone! It didn't seem possible.

"It's Mrs. George Lovell," the first woman answered. "That dog of yours is over here on Third Street digging in my azaleas again. I have tried to be patient, but I feel to warn you . . ." There was a moment of crackling silence.

"Who's there? You can all just hang up, if you don't mind."

"What?" Mrs. Detweiler shouted. "Hang up, you say?"

"No, no, no. Whoever's on the line, hang up, for heaven's sake."

Rose heard three quick *plop*s. She ought to have hung up, but she was mesmerized.

"All right, that's better," Mrs. Lovell said.

"You best send your wages man over here right quick and get this dog of yours, or there'll be trouble, Velma. I am at my wits' end. When my husband gets wind . . ."

Wilder grabbed the receiver out of Rose's hand and held it against his own ear. He listened, wide-eyed, for a long minute; then he took his hand off the mouthpiece and barked and whined into it. Then, with a laugh, he slammed the receiver back in its place.

Rose burst out laughing. Wilder giggled so hard, he almost fell off the chair. Rose was wiping tears from her eyes when the door swung open and E.J. appeared in her dressing sacque. Her graying hair was down, falling over one shoulder, and her eyes were puffy.

"Wilder Thayer, have you been fooling with that contraption again?"

"No, Mother," Wilder lied, trying to smother a chuckle.

"Of course you were," E.J. said matter-of-factly.

Rose blushed hard, not so much at herself,

but at Wilder's bold lying. Yet E.J. hardly seemed to notice. She was never as strict with Wilder as Mama had been with Rose.

"Rose, dear, you mustn't encourage the boy. The telephone is not a toy."

"Yes, E.J.," Rose said as soberly as she could. "I'm sorry."

"And eavesdropping isn't my notion of good manners. Now, who was talking?"

"Mrs. Detweiler's dog got loose again."

E.J.'s eyebrows flew up. "Again? Whose garden did he get into this time?"

"Mrs. Lovell's," Rose answered. "He was digging in her azaleas."

"Land sakes," E.J. said, shuffling sleepily across the kitchen to pour herself a glass of water from the faucet. "I should think Mrs. Lovell was fit to be tied. Those azaleas are her pride and joy. And she's not one to mince her words."

A growl of thunder rumbled in the distance. "You'd better go out and unhook the wire, Wilder. Take Rose with you, to show her how. Sounds as if we'll have a storm this afternoon.

We could use a cooling rain."

Rose followed Wilder out the kitchen door into the backyard. Near to where the telephone wire came out of the house, there was a metal pole in the ground. At the pole, the wire had been cut. The end coming from the house had been bent into a hook. The end coming from the telephone pole had been bent into a loop, which was attached to the pole.

Wilder told Rose to take the hook out of the loop and hang it from a nail sticking out of the house, so the wire wouldn't lie on the ground.

"The lightning can come right down the wire into the house," Wilder explained. "Or even out the ground, if the wire's lying there. Some folks's had their whole house burn up from it."

Another rumble of thunder rolled across the darkening sky. Doors slammed at nearby houses as women dashed out to fetch their wash off the line, and get their hens into their coops.

The idea of a bolt of lightning coming into the house scared Rose. She promised herself she'd never leave it empty until she was sure the telephone had been unhooked.

After that, Rose listened every chance she could. There was no one for her to call up, but every time she was in the kitchen and E.J. wasn't around, she'd pick up the phone just to see if anyone was talking. Often as not, someone was.

Sometimes all the women secretly listening on the line would start talking. But mostly they just listened. The telephone was a great convenience, but you couldn't ever have a private conversation.

Even if no one was talking, Rose would sometimes listen to the hissing, crackling sounds of the wires. It was some kind of magic, the telephone. It defeated distance and erased space, altogether and all at once.

She had read in the newspapers that it was possible to call long distance, all the way across America, from New York to San Francisco, and even to Europe, through a cable laid on the ocean floor. Two people could be separated by half the world, yet talk as if they were sitting across a table.

As she listened to the bristling silence, Rose imagined the wire she was connected to going from pole to pole all across America, and across the Atlantic Ocean. She was connected to the whole world through the thin electric thread.

Even more fantastic was the wireless. Last winter, President Roosevelt had actually exchanged greetings across the Atlantic Ocean by wireless telegraph with Edward VII, King of England. Somehow sparks of electricity could fly around the world and be plucked from the air by anyone with a wireless sounder key. It was astonishing to Rose how much things had changed just in her short life.

On Friday morning, while they were having their breakfast, the fish cart came by. Before Rose had even heard the bell, Viola said, "Fish man's in the street, Mrs. Thayer."

E.J. got her purse and gave Viola some coins. "See if he has some of those nice big shrimp," she told Viola. "If he does, get a dozen, but don't overpay. And get a good piece of fish. We'll have a gumbo."

Rose wanted to see the fish cart, so she went out with Viola when they heard the bell close by.

"Fish! *Poisson!* Fish! *Poisson! Très frais!*" cried the fish hawker, standing at the endgate of his wagon. A small crowd of black women huddled around him, eyeing the fresh fish. He wore a wide straw hat, a blue kerchief around his neck, and overalls.

The women chattered like jaybirds. They were arguing with the fish hawker and laughing at the same time. Rose couldn't understand what they were saying.

"They're fussin' about the prices," said Viola.

"I can't make out a word," Rose said in wonderment. "What is a *'pwah-song'*?"

"That's French for fish. Mr. Chappuis, he hardly speaks a word of English."

Rose stood by, unsure of herself, while Viola waited her turn. She was fascinated to watch these women, some of whom were as blue-black as coal, others so light-skinned they were almost white.

Everyone in that neighborhood, it seemed, had a hired girl. All the girls were brightly dressed, with bandannas on their heads, and they all seemed to enjoy each other's company, laughing and talking with gusto. But when it was their turn to barter with Mr. Chappuis, they put on stern faces.

In the back of the wagon lay wooden crates full of ice, with fish carefully arranged in rows on top. Then a thin layer of ice chips had been sprinkled on top. There were piles of glistening fresh crabs, still stirring, and shrimp, with long catlike whiskers.

When it was Viola's turn, she pointed at the shrimp. *"Combien?"* she asked. There weren't many shrimp left, maybe two dozen.

The fish hawker ignored the shrimp and pointed to a big pile of red-scaled fish and said something.

Viola shook her head and scowled. "No, no," she said, her fists on her hips. And they began to argue. Mr. Chappuis kept pointing to those fish, and to other crates of fish. He waved his hands, and made faces of disgust and disbelief.

Finally he shrugged, and sold Viola the fish she wanted. Then he sold her the shrimp, after some more arguing. He gave her ice to put in the market basket, which she had lined with a kitchen towel. Then the fish and shrimp went into the basket, and then more ice.

By the time it was all done, both Viola and Mr. Chappuis were laughing. Rose was bewildered.

"Well, how did we do?" E.J. asked when they had returned.

"He wanted me to take that snapper, but their eyes were all cloudy. He said, 'Take the snapper. I'll give you a good price and your missus will never know.' He said, 'You keep the money for yourself.' '*Ôte ça dans to colo-quinte*—get that notion out of your head,' I say. Shame on him. I got a nice fresh grouper, and a dozen shrimp like you wanted, Mrs. Thayer."

Viola began cooking up the seafood gumbo as soon as breakfast was done. The kitchen filled with the rich, spicy scents of garlic, peppers, shallots, onions, okra, and salt pork. Viola browned a chicken back and put that in as well. She cooked up a pot of rice, and that also went in. Then she added a bit of filé, ground sassafras, to thicken it. A gumbo had a bit of everything in it. It had a perfect name.

Rose insisted on helping, and Viola let her chop up the onions and shallots.

"Why do they call it gumbo?" asked Rose.

"It's a Creole way to say 'okra,'" Viola said, holding her head back from the spattering meat.

"What is Creole?"

"Creole is a mix-up of French and Spanish, and sometime nigra," she said.

"Are you Creole, Viola?"

Viola laughed, shook her head, and clucked. "Child, you ask too many questions. No, I'm not Creole. Creoles are light-skinned kind of

74

Negroes. I'm just plain old nigra, with a bitty-bit of French. Now hush, child, and chop those onions. I'm almost ready for them."

At dinner Rose's first taste of gumbo set her tongue afire, brought tears to her eyes, and made her break out in a sweat. E.J., Wilder, and Viola had a good laugh at her expense as she gulped milk to cool her tongue. The gumbo had cayenne pepper in it.

"You'll get accustomed to it, in time," E.J. said.

"It's very good," Rose choked. And after the fire went out, it did taste good. But she took smaller sips of the broth.

She had been in Louisiana only a few days, and already she had so much to write about to Mama and Papa and Paul that she hardly knew where to begin.

Odd One Out

"*Amo, amas, amat, amamus, amatis, amant.*"
Rose shut her eyes and translated the Latin words in her head: I love; you love; he, she, or it loves; we love; you (plural) love; they love.

Next verb: *porto, portas, portat . . .* I carry; you carry; he, she, or it carries . . .

Rose sat in one of the comfortable armchairs in Professor Stover's office, trying to concentrate on her first-year Latin text. She was nervous. She remembered one of Papa's favorite expressions: as jumpy as a cat in a room full of rocking chairs. That was exactly how she felt.

She had fussed with her hair so long, she'd been late to school, the last one to arrive on the first day. She decided to part her hair in the middle and draw it back at the sides, just barely covering her ears. Then she plaited it into a single braid, which she coiled and pinned at the back.

She used to pull her hair straight back into a braid, and then she had tried the Gibson Girl look, piled up into a pompadour. But she thought her forehead was just too big and broad, too childish. So she took up this new style to cover part of her forehead, and to make her look a little bit older. Even so, she still had the chubbiest cheeks, like a baby. Sometimes Rose just hated the way she looked.

She had gotten herself into such a state she'd made herself late. She didn't know where to go, so she rushed to Professor Stover's office. She was shocked to find six other scholars there. Everyone in the room stopped talking and stared at her for a long embarrassed moment. There was no place to hide.

Finally Professor Stover introduced Rose.

"Miss Wilder has come to us all the way from Missouri, where her mother and father keep an apple orchard. Do I have that correct?"

Rose nodded.

"She is visiting with her aunt, Mrs. E. J. Thayer, while she completes her studies here. I'm sure you will all welcome her into our little family, Crowley's first high school class."

The other students introduced themselves. Everyone was very polite and refined: "Pleased to meet you." "You are very welcome." "Do you find Crowley to your liking?"

"Yes, I like it very well," Rose answered. She blushed under their inquiring gazes. Then they all sat down and waited for Professor Stover to begin. He leaned against the edge of his desk.

"I will conduct two hours of instruction each day, one in the morning and one in the evening," he said. "The rest of the time you will be on your own, or studying together. You have all been chosen because you are of outstanding character, aptitude, intelligence, and diligence.

"If you want knowledge, you must toil for it. What you will not teach yourselves, you will never learn. The matter is in your hands."

Professor Stover said the students would be expected to honor the rules and observe proper behavior on their own, without being told. He called it the honor system and everyone must agree to abide by it, or they would be asked to leave the school.

Then he handed out their Latin texts and told them all to begin with the first chapter. He gave all the students their third-year texts, and to Rose he gave a first-year book. Then he left.

The three boys—Ivan Way, Richard Schultz, and Vernon Haupt—all sat at one table. The three girls—Carrie Naftel, Mary Holt, and Phala Baur—sat at another. They all had their noses in their books, translating Cicero's first oration against Catiline into their notebooks. The only sound was the turning of pages and the scratching of pencils.

Three boys, three girls—and Rose. She was the odd one out, an outsider in every sense. They all had known each other through most of their schooling. And in Latin, at least, she was as far behind them as a toddler just learning to walk.

Old feelings came back to haunt Rose. She had always been the outsider, as long as she could remember. In her first years in school in Mansfield, she was a poor country girl from a poor farm family. She'd been ashamed of her mended dresses and shoes. She ate her dinner alone so the other children wouldn't see that she had only bacon fat on her bread because Mama and Papa couldn't pay for butter.

After they moved into town, Rose still felt different. She envied the girls who had many dresses and fancy hats and gold bracelets. She was just as smart as they were, smarter even. But she could never be a part of their world. Only Blanche Coday, the druggist's daughter, had become Rose's friend. Even so, it took a few years of knowing Blanche before they became true friends who would share their secrets and their worries.

The words on the page turned blurry as a wave of sadness swept over her. She missed the sound of Mama's voice, the smell of Papa's pipe, the sight of Fido sprawled in front of the heater stove. She missed the comforting rhythms of family life. She was homesick.

She missed Paul terribly, and, as she sat there, she knew for certain that the moment he asked her to marry him, she would say yes. It was hard to be different alone. She saw in Paul the same awkwardness she felt and her same sober way of thinking.

They knew each other as well as if they had been brother and sister. Yet they liked each other so much more than that. Why had she been so determined to go to high school? What was the difference whether she knew how to translate Cicero, or calculate the area of an isosceles triangle? What was the good of it?

With all her studies, she would still marry Paul, settle down, and have a house full of children. If she wanted work, she could always learn telegraphy. She had already taught herself Morse code.

Rose sighed. She had come all this way, and everyone was counting on her to do her best, and on the very first day her heart was fading. She couldn't just up and walk out of school, the way she had done at home. She couldn't go home, where Mama would cluck with disapproval at first, then allow her to stay and study on her own.

E.J. had gone to so much trouble. If for nothing else, she must succeed to show E.J. that her faith in Rose was not wasted.

She flipped the pages of her text. The book fell open to the introduction. She read the first sentence: "The study of Latin will make you an heir to a treasure that neither moth nor rust can corrupt, nor thieves break in and steal."

Such a beautiful way to say it, she thought. She turned to the first chapter. At the top of the page was a Latin saying: "*Post proelium, praemium.* After the battle, the reward."

"Nothing worth having was ever gotten

without a struggle." That was one of Mama's favorite expressions. Here it was, still alive after thousands of years of history. Rose knew she could not let herself give in to an attack of defeatism. She must fight back.

She sighed heavily and started in again: *aqua* = water; *femina* = woman; *natura* = nature. Maybe it wouldn't be so hard after all. Many of the words looked much like English and had the same or similar meanings.

By the time the noon dinner bell rang, Rose was already writing sentences in Latin, and had learned that many of the English words for the months of the year were named for Roman emperors and gods, and the rest came from Roman numbers.

Everyone put away their books and left for their homes. None of the other students asked her to walk with them, so Rose walked back to E.J.'s by herself. School would take up again at three o'clock.

It had rained in the morning, and now a blustery wind blew across the broad open playing fields around the school. She had to hold her skirts down, but it felt good to be out in the fresh air.

Mud puddles speckled the street. Low gray clouds scudded across the sky. The walk from school was eleven blocks long—seven down and four across. She had a choice of ways. She could walk down Parkerson to Fourth Street. She could walk across Tenth Street and down Avenue H. She could zigzag any way she wanted, and they would all be the same distance.

But the scenery would be different. Rose liked having choices. It was something she didn't like about Mansfield. There was one way to do everything, and everywhere she went, she saw the same faces. She had begun to wonder lately if she could live that way all her life, like a mule plowing the same field year after year.

She decided to walk all the way down Parkerson, drawn by the noise and movement of the downtown business district. The life of the city helped pull her out of her gloom.

The courthouse was closing for dinner, and

people poured from the doors like bees from a hive. Some of them had lined up at a hand-cart parked at the corner. A man was selling some kind of food and shouting, "Hot tamales! Get your hot tamales!" She lingered near enough to see that it was something wrapped up in corn shucks.

She walked down the blocks of stores along the wide street, mincing across the clinging mud at the intersections, and feeling shy as she weaved her way down the sidewalks through the shoppers, tradespeople, and running children.

Crowley was such a big city that it had two pharmacies, two milliners, a steam laundry, and more dry goods stores than she could count. She paused before the display windows to gaze longingly at shoes, hats, bottles of perfume, bicycles, cut glassware, furniture—everything and anything a body could desire. When she passed a barbershop, she looked straight ahead. It was improper for a woman to gawk at a man getting a shave.

Although there were many black people on

the street, she saw none in most of the stores. She wondered where they took their trade, where they found their necessities.

She crossed the street to avoid passing by a saloon and was greeted by the smell of baking bread. She spotted the bakery and lingered at the front door, enjoying herself for a moment. Then, without thinking, she walked inside.

The walls and ceiling and counters were all white and sparkling clean. It was hot in there. Behind the counter were bins full of long, narrow loaves of bread. On racks were pies and cakes and pastries. A man in a white apron was tying string around a cake box. Behind him, through a doorway, Rose could see racks and racks of baked goods, and the big doors of the ovens.

Rose was hungry. She had ten cents in her purse. She was wondering what she could pay for when she was startled by a girl's voice behind her.

"Pardon me, miss. May I 'elp you?"

A girl with dark blond hair, about Rose's age, leaned on a broom, smiling.

"Yes, thank you. Can you tell me, how much are the long loaves?" The girl was very pretty, with clear blue eyes. She was dressed simply, in a plain white waist and black skirt. Her hair was pulled straight back, braided and wound into a chignon.

"The breads, they are five cents." The girl had an accent that sounded a bit Southern, but something else, too, the way the girl had dropped the "h" in "help."

"Thank you very much," Rose said. "I will take one, please."

The girl went behind the counter, wrapped one of the honey-brown-colored loaves in a piece of paper, and handed it to Rose. She put a nickel on the counter and was about to turn and leave when the girl said, "*Bonum diem.*"

Rose blinked in confusion. The girl smiled at her expectantly.

"You are a student of Latin, yes?" the girl finally said.

"Yes. I am in Professor Stover's class, at the high school. But how in the world did you know?"

The girl laughed and her eyes sparkled. "You are carrying a Latin text."

Then Rose burst out laughing. Of course— she had it in her hand. "What does it mean, *bonum diem?* I am only just beginning my studies."

"'Good day,'" the girl said. "I am a student of Latin also, at St. Michael's."

"Is that in Crowley?" Rose wondered. She had not heard of any other schools.

"Oh, yes," she said. "It is a school for Catholics."

"Oh," Rose said. She had never met a Catholic person before. Rose's family were Methodists. There was no Catholic church in Mansfield.

Several people came through the door. "You must excuse me," the girl said. "I 'ave customers. *Rursus vene.*"

The girl had such a twinkle in her eye that Rose had to laugh.

"'Come again,'" the girl translated.

"Yes," Rose said, smiling. "Thank you. And *bonum diem* to you as well."

The bread smelled so good, and Rose was so hungry, that she began pulling off chunks and eating it as she walked the rest of the way home. She had never tasted bread that was so light and fragrant, with a crisp, crumbly crust. She promised herself that she would stop and buy bread from that girl again.

Help lift up the common man, for the common good! Join the Social Democratic Party.

HOW LONG MUST WOMEN WAIT?

Something to Believe In

"I'm going tomorrow evening to the Opera House to pass out dodgers," E.J. said, setting a plate of cold leftover chicken on the kitchen table. "Why don't you come and help?"

Rose poured hot water from the kettle into the teapot and brought it to the table, and they all sat down to supper. Viola went home to her own family in the evenings, so supper was almost always leftovers from dinner.

"Dodgers?" asked Rose.

"It's a'verstisements for socialmisms,"

Wilder blurted through a mouthful of cold fried potato.

E.J. frowned at him. "Don't speak with your mouth full, dear. They are announcements, handbills, promoting the cause of socialism and women's rights. Writings by the leaders of progessive thinking. I try to get to the Opera House each night they have a show, and hand them out to the patrons as they arrive. Wilder helps, too, don't you, dear?"

"I want to, very much," Rose answered without skipping a beat. Passing out dodgers to strangers in front of the Opera House sounded very exciting. She couldn't imagine Mama ever doing a thing like that, or allowing Rose to.

She had known for some time that E.J. was a socialist. E.J. belonged to a new political party, the Social Democrats. Mr. Eugene V. Debs was the leader of the Social Democrats. He had been a candidate for president in 1900, and would probably be again next year, in 1904, against President Teddy Roosevelt.

Rose liked President Roosevelt, especially because last winter he had refused to shoot a bear cub that some gamekeepers had brought for him to hunt. After that, some people began making and selling toy bears called Teddy's Bears.

E.J. liked Mr. Debs for president. He believed that all working people should join together in unions to fight the owners of the big companies, the trusts, and the wealthy interests.

Every day in the newspapers there was talk about the evils of the company trusts that seemed to control everything in the country, from shoes to tobacco to oil. The men who owned the trusts got richer and richer while the men, women, and children who worked in their factories and mines lived no better than slaves.

Socialists believed that when the working people would join hands, it would be the greatest force for change in the country. Socialism was coming all over the world. The days when the ruling classes could dictate to the rest of the people were coming to an end.

The socialists also believed in suffrage for women. Women should have the right to vote, which they had in only a few states in America. Rose agreed with the socialists, although she was horrified by the riots and killings that seemed to follow them around.

She was ardent about suffrage. She believed that though men might earn the most money, women did the most work.

"But I mustn't stay out too long, E.J. I have my Latin to keep up, and Professor Stover gave us two pages of plane geometry problems to solve."

The evening light had faded, so E.J. reached over and turned up the wick on the coal-oil lamp. The newspaper, *The Crowley Signal*, had said there would be no electric lights that night. The generator had broken down, and the parts to fix it must be sent from New Orleans. The electric generating plant was always breaking down.

"We won't be long," E.J. assured her. "Just

as long as it takes for folks to arrive at the show. We'll come straight home after."

All the next day at school Rose looked forward with excitement and nervousness to the evening. She hurried home in a pouring rain at dinnertime, not even stopping to buy bread, so she could get a leg up on her studies.

That night after supper, E.J., Wilder, and Rose walked to the Opera House. The front of the Opera House blazed with electric lights. Everything glittered. Colorful posters announced that there would be a show of minstrelsy that night with sentimental ballads, comedy, and lively dances.

The street was cluttered with buggies and horses, and the sidewalk thronged with people dressed in their Sunday best. Rose's heart pounded, but little Wilder seemed perfectly at home.

E.J. talked to two women who were already passing out dodgers. E.J. took a stack, gave some to Rose, and handed a small stack to

Wilder. The headline on the dodger read: "Help Lift Up the Common Man for the Common Good! Join the Social Democratic Party." Underneath it was a smaller headline: "How Long Must Women Wait?"

Under the headlines was an article by Mr. Debs, and below that an announcement of a meeting for those interested in the socialist cause.

"You be the perfect little gentleman, now," E.J. warned Wilder.

"What should I do?" Rose asked.

"Take one," E.J. said, taking one of the dodgers, "and hold it out to anyone who comes by. Just say something polite, like 'Please take one.' Just keep handing them out 'til they are gone."

Then E.J. marched off to begin. Rose watched her and the other women for a minute. She did not feel comfortable talking to men, so she picked a woman who was by herself. She stuck out her hand with the piece of paper in it and whispered, "Please, won't you take one?"

The woman took it without a word, looked at it for an instant, then handed it back and walked into the Opera House. Rose stood there for a moment, stunned. She couldn't do this. She couldn't make a spectacle of herself, and let people look at her like some curiosity in the circus.

She was shrinking back into the shadows when a man in a derby hat and boiled collar walked right up to her. She froze in terror. The man smiled. He shifted a gold-headed cane from his right hand to his left and looked at her quizzically. A stud on his shirtfront gleamed in the bright light.

"May I have one?" he finally asked.

"Yes," Rose managed to croak. "Yes, of course." She fumbled with the stack and then dropped all the dodgers. They scattered like leaves. "Oh, dear!" Rose cried out.

They knelt down at the same time.

"Please," the man said gently. "Allow me."

Rose stood, mortified, while the man gathered up all her dodgers. She wanted to run, to be anywhere but there. Crowds of people had begun to arrive, and some of them were staring at her as they walked into the Opera House. Rose caught E.J.'s eye and shrugged helplessly. E.J. raised one eyebrow.

When he had the dodgers all together, the man tidied them up, took one, and handed the rest to Rose. She stood, her tongue tied in a knot, while he read the page. With his head bowed, she could study him without his noticing.

He was crisply dressed, with patent leather shoes, and pants with razor-sharp creases, and a black silk stripe down the outside of each leg. He had hooked the handle of his cane over his left arm. The handle was carved in the shape of a swan's head, and it glittered in the bright electric lights. She detected the faint scent of cigar smoke.

He was much older than Rose, but she could tell he was still a young man by the smooth skin on his cheeks.

"This is very interesting," he said. "Do you yourself hold that women ought to have the vote?"

"Yes," Rose said quietly. There was something gentle in his eyes that gave her courage. "I do believe it with all my heart. Women are as intelligent as men, and should have some voice in the government of our country."

He smiled. "But women cannot bear arms in defense of our country."

"No, they cannot," Rose agreed. "But women bear the sons who bear the arms."

The electric lights blinked once, and a voice called out from inside the doors: "It's showtime, folks. Showtime. Please find your seats. The show is about to begin."

The man smiled again. "That is a good answer. I think you will make a fine suffragist. Good evening to you." He tipped his hat.

"Good evening," Rose said. The man turned and disappeared into the Opera House.

Rose let out the big breath she'd been holding. She had surprised herself with her courage. Her fears melted away, and she plunged into the crowd, stood next to E.J., and began passing out her dodgers.

In a few minutes the audience had moved

inside, and most of the dodgers were gone. A few discarded ones fluttered about on the sidewalk.

Rose was exhilarated as they walked home. She thought about the man in the derby. He was the fanciest dresser she'd ever seen, a rich man for certain. And he had looked at Rose in a way no boy ever had, not even Paul Cooley. She wondered what it meant.

She was so flushed with excitement that it didn't occur to her until later, as she lay under the tester in the dark of her bedroom, that passing out dodgers, and debating with that man, had been one of the most important things she'd ever done in her life. She was advancing the cause of her fellow man—and woman, she remembered to think.

She'd never felt so strong and independent. She would make a fine suffragist. His words echoed over and over again in her head.

Rose swelled with pride; she had found something to believe in. She could devote her heart and soul to it, and that would change her forever.

Bayou Country

Dearest daughter Rose,

Can it be a month you are gone, and still we have not heard so much as a peep? Thank heavens for Eliza Jane's kind letters, or we should wonder that you had fallen off the face of the earth!

Autumn is full upon the Ozarks. Last night Papa and I rode the horses out to the farm. We climbed to the top of the rise above the spring and counted eight brush fires burning on the hills to the south. It was such a pretty night, with an orange moon floating up from the horizon. But I will never trust these farmers

*to be careful after nearly losing our own place
in that awful fire.*

Rose's stomach flopped from guilt. She had
been so busy with school and her new life.
She had kept promising herself that she would
write Mama and Papa, but when she had the
will, she hadn't the time. When she had
the time, she was either too tired, or there was
so much to tell that she didn't know where
to begin.

"Dearest Mama and Papa," she finally
wrote.

*I have been a bad girl to wait so long to
write. Of course I am well. I am very happy
here, as Crowley is such a large city with people
of many different persuasions and cultures.*

Rose described her night in front of the
Opera House, knowing Mama would be
shocked that E.J. let her do such a thing. No
one in Mansfield would ever think to stand

on a public street talking to strangers about politics. She did leave out the part about the man. Mama would think E.J. had completely lost her senses.

Rose thought differently. She had become so fond of E.J. She seemed very young, and had lived an exciting, independent life.

Rose had heard many of Mama's stories about growing up on the unsettled prairies of the Middle West. She had heard about the hardships of farming in that new land. But E.J. had been a pioneer farmer by herself, without a husband and children to help. Only Papa and her other brothers had helped her now and again. E.J. had emigrated from Minnesota to Dakota Territory before there was even a railroad.

"I was the great enthusiast, as we all were," E.J. explained one day over dinner. "I counted the hardships as nothing against the happiness of having made a home for myself."

E.J. had learned to pound nails, laying the floor herself and putting on the shingles. She had nearly died picking poisonous bean bugs off her potato plants. She had even slept with two loaded revolvers under her pillow, the country was so wild.

"Weren't you a brave young thing!" Viola cried, filling a basket with corn bread. "I don't even like to go out by the bayous in the night."

"'Foolish' would be a better word for it," E.J. said. "I nearly killed myself several times over, and ruined my health for good and all."

The prairie weather had been so harsh, it was nearly impossible to raise a good crop, or even keep a cow alive. E.J. had taken an agency for a bookseller, traveling thousands of miles on the railroads selling books to earn the money to keep up her little farm.

Finally E.J. had had to admit it was impossible for her to continue homesteading by herself. She sold her place and went to Washington, D.C., where she took a position as a government girl in the Department of the Interior, working in an office.

She became friends with Dr. Mary Walker, the first woman surgeon in the War Between the States. And she had been friends with Mrs. Amelia Bloomer, a pioneer of suffragism and dress reform for women.

"I admired them both so," E.J. said. Dr. Walker had taken to wearing men's suits and was always getting herself arrested for it. Mrs. Bloomer had dressed in pants that buttoned at the ankles, with tunics and wide hats. Bloomers had been named for her.

"I never had quite the courage to dress as they did," E.J. said, laughing. "Those two had a big effect for women. You can't know, Rose, how awful it was to wear hoopskirts, as I did when I was a girl. You could hardly pass through a doorway without getting yourself stuck, and sitting down was impossible."

Rose sat in raptured silence, hardly touching her food, as E.J. talked about Washington and how ordinary it was to see the famous and important men of the day, even President Harrison, strolling the streets of the capital.

"Why did you leave Washington?" Rose wondered. "It sounds wonderfully exciting."

"Family," E.J. said simply. "I missed

Mother and Father, and everyone else, too. So I went back to Minnesota to their farm, and that is where I met Mr. Thayer and we were married."

One Sunday after church, Rose's uncle Perley came to pick them up in his wagon and take them all out to his farm for dinner. Grandmother Wilder was living there as well. Uncle Perley was E.J.'s brother, and Papa's, too. He and Aunt Elsie lived on a rice farm on the Mermentau River, about ten miles from Crowley.

"Well, well," Uncle Perley said when he arrived. "I finally get to meet Manzo's little girl, all grown up." Papa's proper name was Almanzo, but his brothers and sisters had always called him Manzo.

It was the first time Rose had seen Uncle Perley since she was a baby, before she could remember. She was shocked at how much he looked like Papa, with the same broad forehead and large nose.

Uncle Perley had more hair than Papa, and

kept his face clean-shaven. He spoke with a lively voice, not quietly like Papa. Mama liked to say that Papa was as tight-lipped as an oyster.

Uncle Perley took them for a long-way-'round ride by Bayou Plaquemine and Bayou Blanc, two swampy rivers that passed near Crowley. Rose saw a lovely farmstead along Bayou Blanc. The two-story house had its stairway on the outside, and in the yard there was a chinaberry tree with a horse tied to it.

Perley said it was an Acadian house, where a family of French settlers lived. Rose asked what an Acadian was, and E.J. told her the tragedy of the French Canadians who were driven out of Canada by the British in the 1750s. Many of them died; families were broken up, and they became scattered in the American colonies. They finally settled in Louisiana when it was still a colony of France. They had kept their language and traditions through all the years.

"They called themselves Arcadians," E.J. explained, "because Arcadia was a beautiful province of Ancient Greece. Perhaps you will learn of it in your Latin studies. Arcadia was made famous by the Roman poet Virgil. The Arcadians were said to lead virtuous, idealistic lives. The English misheard the word, and now they are called Acadians."

Bayou was an Acadian word for "small river," E.J. said, and the Acadians borrowed it from a Choctaw word for river—*bayuk*. Bayou Blanc meant White River. Bayou Plaquemine meant Burned Persimmon River.

Rose's head was filling with languages, and she had begun making connections between them. The Latin word for river was *flumen*. Everywhere Uncle Perley drove them, they saw flumes, long wooden aqueducts that brought water from the bayous and rivers to the rice fields.

Pumps driven by gasoline engines raised the water up into the flumes, and then gravity carried it along the flumes to the rice fields. The whole flat country was covered with curving fields of slender rice stalks ready to be harvested. The fields looked much like fields of young wheat, but less crowded.

Here and there they passed fields of sugarcane, and cotton, too. The cotton had bloomed, and the branches were covered with puffy white cotton bolls. The bushes looked as if there had just been a heavy, wet snow, with bits of it still clinging to the leaves.

Uncle Perley pointed out pecan orchards and even a stand of orange trees, although the oranges had long ago been picked.

Uncle Perley *whoa*ed the horses on the bank of Bayou Plaquemine, and they got down from the wagon for a few minutes to look around. Trees cloaked in Spanish moss hugged the shore. Enormous cypress trees, with their roots under water, soared high above the dark, murky swamp.

A shallow boat had been pulled up on the bank, and there were piles of moss along the shore that Perley said had been harvested for stuffing pillows and furniture.

In the dark shady places the water was choked with flowering purple hyacinths. The mat of green looked solid enough to walk across, like a living quilt.

"You wouldn't dare to try," Uncle Perley said. "There are all kinds of poison snakes in there, and even alligators."

"Look, there's one!" Wilder shouted. At the same moment, Rose felt a jab in the back. She jumped and shrieked. Wilder giggled.

"You little scamp!" she cried out. She chased and easily caught him, pulling on his ear until he begged for mercy.

After that they drove to Perley's house. Aunt Elsie had a brand-new baby boy. He was named James, after Grandfather Wilder. Rose hardly recognized Grandmother Wilder. It had been many years since Rose had seen her in Mansfield, when she and Grandfather Wilder came for a summer visit. But Rose did remember her big puff of snow-white hair that she had twisted into a knot. She remembered her dancing eyes and her fluttering hands.

Now Grandmother sat in an easy chair in the parlor, too weak to stand and walk without help, her eyes tired, her spirit listless. Rose placed a light kiss on her withered cheek. E.J. had told Rose that Grandmother had never been the same since Grandfather had died.

Both of Rose's grandfathers had gone to their reward, and Rose could see that Grandmother Wilder would soon follow them. Then her only grandparent left would be Grandma Ingalls, and Rose might never see her again; she lived so far away.

Growing old was a cruel trick of life, she thought. Someday Mama and Papa would be old, and then . . . She was glad when Elsie handed her little James to hold and she could brush the sad thoughts from her mind.

"You ought to write and tell your father how well we are doing down here," Uncle Perley said at dinner. "Maybe you could persuade him to bring your mother down. We miss him, and the climate would do them both good. We get two gardens out of each growing season, and there's plenty of opportunity for a fellow that wants it."

"That would be nice, Uncle Perley," Rose

agreed. She thought Papa would like Louisiana very much. "But Mama is determined never to move again. And what Mama wants, Mama gets."

"I reckon you're right about that," Perley said, chuckling. "Man has his will, but woman has her way."

After dinner Perley took them for a walk over his fields. He showed Rose the irrigation canal, and the ditches that brought the water to his fields for planting. In the spring, after the rice sprouted, the fields must be kept flooded. Rice was a crop that did best in very damp soil. Each field had a dike all the way around it, to keep the water from running off. Perley said the soil had a natural clay pan under it, so dense that water couldn't seep through it.

"In the old days they planted Providence rice," Uncle Perley explained. "If Providence sent the rain, it filled the dikes and the farmer got his rice. But now we don't have to depend on the weather."

Now that harvesttime was near, the water

had been drained from the fields. The rice stalks were golden brown, with heavy drooping grain heads.

It seemed to Rose that Louisiana was as rich as the horn of plenty, giving the best of the land and the sea all in one place. It was easy to understand why so many folks had come from other parts of the country to settle there.

Rose did miss the hills of home. Louisiana could never hold a candle to the beauty of the Ozarks. But she found herself becoming so contented in Crowley that it was hard to imagine going back when school was finished. There was more to life than a pretty landscape.

The Social Democrats

O ne day Rose decided to take some of E.J.'s dodgers for the Social Democrats to school, to give them to the other scholars. But when there was a chance, she lacked the courage. It seemed easier to hand them out to strangers.

But on her way home from school, stopping at the bakery to buy bread, she pressed one into the hand of the girl behind the counter. Week by week they had become more friendly.

The girl's name was Odile Boudreaux. She had written her name down for Rose to see, and taught her how to say it: "Boo-droh." She was Acadian, Rose had learned, and her uncle Jean-Claude was the baker.

Each day they had a short conversation, as long as Odile was not too busy. Odile had taught Rose a few French words and phrases: *Bonjour* meant "hello." To say "Thank you," Rose learned to say *Merci*. If she added *beaucoup*, she had said "Thank you very much."

"*Bonjour*, Rose." The shop was empty. Odile swept bread crumbs from the counter with a whisk broom.

"*Bonjour*, Odile. *Comment allez-vous?* How are you?"

"*Bien*," Odile said, plucking a nice, un-crushed bread from the bin behind her. "I am well. *Et vous?*"

"*Très bien*. I am very well."

Rose pulled the dodger from her purse, un-folded it, and laid it on the counter, smoothing the creases.

"Odile, I want to give this to you. It is a

114

notice of a meeting of the Social Democrats, next Thursday evening, upstairs at Ellis's Hardware Store."

Rose quickly explained that the Social Democrats were for the common man, and for women's right to vote.

Odile's eyebrows flew up. "You would like to vote, yes?"

"Why, yes, of course," Rose said, putting her nickel on the counter. "Women have just as much intelligence as men. Why shouldn't we have a say in the government?"

Odile looked at the dodger for a moment. "Me, I don't think I could go to such a meeting," she said slowly. "In my family, the women, they do not care to vote. Thank you very much."

"But whyever not?" Rose insisted. "Don't you think we girls should have the same choice as a man?"

Odile shrugged, still studying the dodger. "It is an interesting idea. Will you go to this meeting yourself?"

"Yes," said Rose. "My aunt Eliza Jane is very active for the cause of socialism and suffragism."

"Me, I don't know. Maybe if . . ."

Just then Odile's uncle came through the swinging door from the back of the bakery, wiping his hands on a towel. Odile quickly snatched the dodger off the counter and crumpled it into her apron pocket before he could see it. She was flustered, so Rose said no more about it.

The next day Odile asked Rose, "Why do you want to vote, Rose? *Ma mère*, my mother, she says it is foolishness for women to stick their noses into men's business. She says no decent woman would want to vote."

"My aunt Eliza Jane would like to vote," Rose countered. "She is a decent woman. It is women who do the most work. You know, 'Man's work ends at setting sun, but woman's work is never done.' Women are partners of men in life. Why not in government as well?"

"Mon Dieu!" Odile said. "If you could 'ear

116

my father speak of it, your ears, they would burn."

Each day they had another slice of conversation. Rose could see that Odile was wrestling in her mind between what she felt in her heart, and what her family believed.

The night of the meeting Rose looked and looked for Odile. She stood by the door with E.J., greeting people as they arrived. She handed out pamphlets of quotations from Eugene V. Debs.

Most of the people who came were women whom E.J. knew through her church. A few of the husbands came, too. But when it was time to sit down and start the meeting, Odile had not arrived. Rose was sorry, because she had hoped for a chance to share her enthusiasm.

The small audience had seated themselves in Mr. Ellis's storeroom. Feed bags and harness equipment were stacked along the walls. Two bare lightbulbs hung from the ceiling, throwing a garish, smokeless light on everything. E.J. stood up to speak, and Rose was just closing the door when she heard a latecomer tromping up the stairs.

She opened it and, to her surprise, saw the man to whom she had given a dodger in front of the Opera House. He took off his hat and smiled at Rose.

"Oh," was all Rose could think to say.

"Good evening," he said. "Is this where the Social Democrats are meeting?"

"Yes," Rose said, recovering her composure. "Yes, of course. We are pleased that you have decided to join us. I am Rose Wilder."

"I am pleased to make your acquaintance," he said. "My name is Isaac Skidmore."

Mr. Skidmore did not have his cane with him, and he wore an everyday suit of clothes. But Rose could see that the cloth was fine wool, and he had a crisp air about him, an elegance and grace.

"Mr. Skidmore, please do come in and have a seat. My aunt, Mrs. Thayer, is about to begin."

Rose sat next to E.J.'s empty chair. Mr.

Skidmore sat behind her. E.J. spoke to the crowd about a gathering that would be held in a few months in the capital city of Louisiana, Baton Rouge, to support women's rights. E.J. said some folks had written to Mr. Debs, asking him to speak there.

"As you all know, we are endeavoring to bring attention to the laws on marital rights in this state, laws which are based on ancient prejudices, and which treat women no better than livestock."

One of the women in the audience raised her hand. "I would like to know why it is that some of our best women, such as Mrs. Carey Thomas, do not speak out more forcefully for our cause. It is common knowledge that she is fully for suffragism. She is in a position to bring attention to it. But she doesn't speak out."

"I do know what you mean," E.J. replied. "But as president of Bryn Mawr College she has spoken out against the curriculum of manners. In time I believe she will become more forceful and speak beyond academics."

Rose had read some of Mrs. Thomas's comments in the newspapers. Mrs. Thomas had written an article against the president of Harvard University, who had argued that education for women should not be much more than learning how to keep house. "The domestic arts," he called it. He was an insult to women, Rose thought.

A man with a fierce frown on his face stood up. "You ladies're putting the cart before the horse!" he cried out. "It's the workingman that needs our help first. If we don't stick to our guns and raise him up, how can he change the women's position?"

Everyone turned to stare at him. Rose caught Mr. Skidmore stealing a sidelong glance at her. She wouldn't return his gaze, but she felt his eyes on her. She straightened her back, and kept her eyes soberly fixed on the man who was speaking.

"If the common man gets the power, it will follow for women as surely as day follows night," the man was saying. "You gals forget that it's the workingman who puts the bread on the table. We're Social Democrats, not Suffrage Democrats."

A shouting match erupted. "Hampton Darville, you know as well as the next one, the power is in the ballot box," a woman retorted.

"It's women who *bake* the bread!" another shouted.

Rose trembled. The room crackled with ill will. It was frightening, even ridiculous, to see grown adults mixed up in a schoolyard argument.

E.J. waded in among the chairs, shushing people until she finally got the room quieted down again. Just before she turned back to the front, Rose caught Mr. Skidmore's eye. He flashed her a conspiratorial grin. She couldn't help smiling back. It *was* sort of humorous. She wondered which side of the argument he took.

The question was never settled. Instead E.J. talked about Mr. Debs and his plans for the next election. She read from some of his writings.

"'Some well-meaning but deluded people think that all wickedness can be overcome by prohibition,'" E.J. read. "'Anything they do not happen to like is bad according to their ethics, and forthwith is put upon the prohibition list.

"'They throw a fit over a man taking a drink or playing a game of cards. But they are not concerned about wage-slavery or child-sweating which have a thousand victims where the saloon has one.'"

Rose felt herself being swept along by his words.

"'It is wonderful how tamely people will consent to this spirit of intolerance, this mean and narrow fanaticism. Speaking for myself, if I were hungry and friendless today, I would rather take my chances with a saloonkeeper than with the average preacher.'"

A shock ran through the audience. An old lady huffed, "Well, I never!" A chair scraped violently.

A man sitting in the back jumped up and stormed out, muttering. They heard him clumping down the stairs, and the door slammed.

E.J. sighed. "Perhaps we should discuss finances. We will be having an ice-cream social to raise money . . ."

The meeting went on a long time, right up until the lights blinked. Everyone hurried to gather their things and say their good-byes before the generating plant closed down.

Rose waited for E.J., who was the last to come out, to join her. Mr. Skidmore walked up to E.J. and introduced himself.

"That was a stimulating discussion. I should like to hear more. I wonder if I might have the honor of escorting you and Miss Wilder to your home?"

"That is very kind, Mr. Skidmore," E.J. said. Rose's stomach fluttered.

They tromped down the wooden stairs and out into the dark street. The pharmacist was just closing up his shop next door, and the few people on the street were hurrying home. The night was quiet except for the katydids chattering in the trees, and the jingle and creak of a passing wagon. This was the coolest evening since Rose had arrived, but still the air felt summery. She was beginning to notice how much longer the mild weather lasted than it did in Missouri.

Mr. Skidmore walked between Rose and E.J., taking each by an arm. Rose thought it a gallant way to stroll. A silver moon hung over the courthouse.

"I wonder, Mrs. Thayer, how you came to be so ardent a follower of Mr. Debs. You speak of him as if he were a saint."

E.J. nodded her head. "In fact, Mr. Skidmore, his followers who personally know him do hero-worship him. He has a smile that could soften the saddest heart, yet his oratory could knock over the Tower of Babel. I saw him speak once, in Washington, D.C., and I have admired his sincerity and simplicity ever since."

"And you, Miss Wilder? Where does your enthusiasm come from?"

"My aunt has been very influential," said Rose, holding up her skirt as they crossed the street. "I am just beginning to study his work. And what is the nature of your interest?"

Mr. Skidmore cleared his throat. "Well, now, I didn't say I had an interest. Not yet, anyway. But the question is before the whole country. Social upheaval cannot be ignored. It is upon everyone's doorstep."

"And the question of suffrage?" E.J. asked. "Where do you stand on it?"

Mr. Skidmore said he thought it was a good idea, but he doubted men would easily give women their freedom.

Then they talked about Louisiana. Rose told him why she was in Crowley. Mr. Skidmore said he lived in Chicago. He was staying with a sister in Crowley while looking into some business interests in the rice trade. He had been in Crowley for just a month, and would be staying on until the spring.

Rose could see that E.J. found Mr. Skidmore charming. He had an intelligent and natural way of speaking. Rose found him charming, too. So, when they reached the gate of E.J.'s house, and he asked Rose if he could see her again, she immediately said, "Yes."

E.J. stiffened. Rose's heart began to pound thickly.

E.J. began, "Rose, dear—"

"Would Sunday after dinner be agreeable?" Mr. Skidmore interrupted. "I could hire a buggy."

"Yes," said Rose. "That would very pleasant."

As soon as they were inside and she had closed the door behind them, E.J. whispered loudly in the darkened house, "Dear Rose. You are a caution sometimes!" She struck a match and lit the hall lamp.

"Do you think it wise to go buggy riding with a complete stranger? We don't know a thing about him." She pulled the pins out of her hat, and hung it on the hall tree.

"We do know something about him," Rose said, pulling off her gloves. "I'm sure he's very kind. He's obviously very refined."

"I can't help it, Rose," said E.J. "You're a big girl, but I'm still beholden to your mother and father to keep you from harm's way. If anything should happen, I—"

"There's no harm in an old buggy ride, E.J. I guess I know how to care for myself." Rose flounced off to her room, giddy with a kind of triumph, and a little bit guilty, too.

For all she knew, Mr. Skidmore might be a traveling man. Traveling men were wicked. When they weren't going from town to town drumming up business in some thing or other, they were trying to ruin the reputations of good, honest girls. Or they just loafed around hotel lobbies smoking cigars and playing cards.

But Mr. Skidmore didn't look the least bit like the traveling men Rose had seen. Besides, she wasn't under Mama's thumb anymore, and E.J. couldn't stop her. She was almost seventeen, for heaven's sake! Why shouldn't she go riding with a cultured, handsome gentleman?

She couldn't wait until Sunday.

Mr. Skidmore

Rose spent four hours riding around Acadia Parish with Mr. Skidmore, but it could have been ten minutes the way the time flew. They never stopped talking. Mr. Skidmore fascinated Rose, and he seemed to find her interesting as well.

They talked about politics, Latin, the great cities, Louisiana. The conversation in the phaeton flowed like water as the shimmering black horses trotted up and down the flat roads. Mr. Skidmore was a good, careful driver, and he never once did a thing to make Rose uncomfortable.

Mr. Skidmore

They stopped in Mermentau for an ice cream and sat on a carriage blanket on the riverbank. They watched a shrimp boat unload its cargo at the dock. The briny odor was strong, but Rose was too intrigued to care. Everything seemed to strike her fancy.

Mr. Skidmore was a college man, Rose learned. He was twenty-four years old. The difference in their ages gave Rose a jolt at first. But she felt older than her years, and they had so many interests in common, she hardly noticed.

Mr. Skidmore enjoyed the study of languages and could speak Greek, Latin, and French as fluently as English. He was a man of business. His father was a banker in Chicago and had sent Isaac to Louisiana to study the rice trade, to see if it held an opportunity for profit.

"So you see, I am one of the enemy." He chuckled.

"You mean a capitalist? But I think you must be a good capitalist." Rose wanted to be agreeable.

"I would like to be just that, when I have my own estate. I should like to be as rich as Andrew Carnegie, and equally generous. That is my notion of lifting up the common man."

Rose pondered that a moment. She watched the shrimp men struggling with a bulging net. It looked like terribly hard work.

"But isn't it true that to be as rich as Mr. Carnegie, one must exploit the working-man?" Rose said. "Wouldn't it be a better thing to increase wages and shorten hours so more folks could have work? I should think that would be an act of generosity that would help people when they need it most. And it isn't charity."

Mr. Skidmore pulled out his handkerchief and dabbed a trickle of ice cream that had melted down Rose's thumb. Rose tensed at first, but she enjoyed his thoughtfulness.

"I don't know if one must exploit the workers," he said. "But I do know what you mean. Sometimes my father sends me to in-spect his interests and holdings. In Chicago I have seen the hatred in the eyes of the

slaughterhouse and factory workers. Your Mr. Debs is a hero in my city, but my father thinks he is the incarnation of the devil. I worry about where the country is going with such fiercely opposing forces."

By the time Mr. Skidmore had dropped Rose back at E.J.'s, they had become cozy friends. E.J. stood in the doorway with her arms folded, watching as Mr. Skidmore helped Rose down from the buggy, shook her hand, and said good-bye.

Rose hesitated at the gate as he climbed back up into the seat.

He picked up the whip and was about to unset the brake when he paused and looked at Rose with questioning eyes. "Miss Wilder, I wonder if I might have the pleasure of driving you to school in the morning?"

"That's very kind of you, but I don't mind the walk at all," Rose said. She wanted to say yes, but didn't want E.J. to see her being too brash.

"I have no obligations, and I would consider it an honor. If the weather is inclement, you might find it a convenience."

Rose glanced at E.J. "I would be very grateful." They set the time, and he drove off.

"Well?" E.J. demanded.

"He was very proper and dignified," Rose said, taking off her boater. "I enjoy his company very well."

"And he's coming again in the morning? I don't know, Rose. It seems rather of a sudden, don't you think?"

Rose sighed. "Oh, E.J. I know you care for me. But I'm not a little girl anymore. Please don't fret so."

"In my day, you'd have just about ruined your good name, gadding about with a man you hardly know."

Rose cared not one whit how of-a-sudden her acquaintance with Mr. Skidmore seemed. She liked him, and she enjoyed his attentions. She had no thought of anything but friendship. After all, her heart belonged to Paul Cooley.

But why shouldn't she have a beau? Why must she sit at home while other girls got courted? And compared with the awkward village boys who had asked to walk her home from church in Mansfield, Mr. Skidmore was a Prince Charming. Rose was not about to give him up so easily.

Now her life took on a new rhythm. Mr. Skidmore drove her to school most mornings, rain or shine. Most evenings after school he was waiting for her, in the buggy with its red wheels and rubber tires.

He drove her to E.J.'s house, where Rose ran in and dropped her books while E.J. paced in the foyer with worry lining her smooth face.

"Be in by nine o'clock," E.J. would call out to Rose's back as she dashed out the door.

And then they drove off for the evening. For the first time in her life, Rose ate in restaurants. She tried every kind of dish, even étouffée, which was made with a giant crawfish that could be caught near the bayous. But she always preferred a good steak, or chicken pie.

Mr. Skidmore

After supper they drove along the dusty white roads in the moonlight; between the cypress trees bearded with moss, past the prickly rice fields, through the sleepy little towns and by the gleaming dark bayous. One night they saw alligators sleeping in a pile along the bank. They looked as harmless as a stack of logs. But Rose was glad they never stirred.

They took to holding hands, and Rose could plainly see that Isaac wanted to kiss her. But she gave him no encouragement. And always, she was back to E.J.'s by nine o'clock.

Then she got down to her work. She quickly changed into a comfortable house-dress and took her books out to a table on the side gallery. It was pleasant out there in the cool evening, now that the steamy mosquito nights had passed. The gallery was jungly, buried in vines, so she could study in privacy.

She began with her Latin translations, a beautiful Roman poem called *The Aeneid*, written by Virgil. She wrote the Latin words down the left side of a sheet of paper. Then she looked up the English words and wrote them on the right side:

Arma	*Arms*
virumque	*and man*
cano,	*I sing,*
Troiae	*of Troy*
qui	*who*
primus	*first*
ab	*from*
oris	*coasts*

Then she would try to make sense of it. Her translation was clumsy, but when Professor Stover showed her the proper phrasing, she was captivated by its beauty:

Arms and the man I sing, who, forced by fate,
And haughty Juno's unrelenting hate,
Expelled and exiled, left the Trojan shore.
Long labors, both by sea and land, he bore.

The Romans plunked their phrases down in the strangest places. But she could see the logic of it and found she could study it almost the way she studied algebra, looking for the rules. In no time at all she was sailing through her Latin translations.

When she had spent too much time on Latin and the words went blank to her, all meaning the same nothing, there was algebra or geometry. And then when her tired brain could no longer hold on to angles and cubic contents, she knew she must allow herself some sleep.

The hours between twelve and two o'clock in the morning were the worst. One night at half past twelve, feeling that she must give in, she took the alarm clock from the kitchen. She wound and reset it by the kitchen clock. Then she threw herself, fully dressed, on the bed.

The alarm rang. She was awake, and clearly in her mind she saw the solution of the geometry problem that had baffled her in her last waking efforts.

Rose seized a pencil and wrote it down. Then she plunged her head into cold water in the wash basin. She drank a cup of stale coffee, and took the clock out to the gallery. She was settling down to work again when she noticed the hands pointing to twelve thirty-five.

What had happened? She must have been so foggy that she set the alarm wrong.

She had slept—how long? Two minutes? And in two minutes of sleep, she had solved the geometry problem.

Trembling with excitement, she went over the solution that she had written. It was correct. She understood it perfectly. She had done it. But how? Did her mind go on working while she slept? Did it work better when she was sleeping?

Maybe she was dreaming. Reality and fantasy were getting mixed up, and her eyes were closing again. With terrific effort she held herself awake and concentrated her attention on the next geometry problem.

When she had grasped it, she set the alarm

two minutes ahead, wound the clock, and put her head down. The alarm rang in her ear; she woke; she had the problem solved.

Look at the next problem and repeat. In fifteen minutes Rose had solved all six problems.

Then she crawled into bed and slept until the alarm woke her to tomorrow and Isaac Skidmore in his shiny phaeton.

How she stayed awake during the days and evenings, she didn't know. But if she thought to have a friendship with any of the other students, she made that impossible by the amount of time she spent with Mr. Skidmore. She was always busy, and when she wasn't, she was too tired to put her charm on.

She enjoyed her studies, enjoyed doing them mostly on her own. That was the way it had been all her school life.

The closest she came to joining with the others was the day one of the boys said an older cousin in college had offered him a Latin "pony." No one knew why they called it that, because the pony was a book. It had many of the great Roman speeches and poems, already translated.

"Do you think it would be right to use it?" he wondered. "I would share it with everyone."

"Maybe if we used it just to help us with our translations," one of the boys suggested.

"If we honestly used it to learn and honestly knew the lessons, it might not be wrong," one of the girls piped up.

The others nodded.

Finally Rose spoke up. "Isn't there something sneaky about that? If we are bound by our honor, isn't that breaking the code if Professor Stover doesn't know of it?"

The rest of the students nodded gravely. They had taken the honor pledge seriously. No one wanted to break it and disappoint everyone else, especially Professor Stover.

"You could ask him," Rose suggested.

But no one wanted to do that. It was sneaky to use it without telling, and certainly Professor Stover would disapprove. So the boy who had been offered the pony refused it.

The rest of the time at school, Rose kept to herself. She had no connection to any of the other students, and she'd be leaving at the end of the school year. Passing time with Mr. Skidmore made her feel wiser as well. She didn't know any of the people they gossiped about, and had no interest in their idle chatter.

She sometimes wished she were a more sociable person. She envied the lively girls who always seemed to have a crowd around them. But Rose was particular about who she passed her time with. Unless she could be with someone interesting or entertaining, she would rather curl up any day with a book.

However, Rose did not intend to be invisible in Crowley High School. Professor Stover had told the class that the scholar who earned the best marks in Latin for the year would have the honor of giving the valedictory speech at graduation. Rose intended to get the best marks in Latin. She would be the valedictorian.

E.J.'s admiration for Eugene Debs had

inspired Rose. Mr. Debs was not an important man because he was sociable. Neither were Mrs. Thomas and all the other women who spoke out for decency and equality. They were important because they could write and say what they believed with such power and conviction that people listened and heard.

Rose was so certain of being the valedictorian that she had even started to form an idea of what she would speak about. She would give her speech about suffragism. She might not be popular like other girls, but she was determined that no one would forget her.

A Real Bad Thing

One cold, rainy Saturday Rose was curled up by the heater stove in the parlor, reading a novel that one of the women in the Social Democratic Party had recommended. It was *The Awakening*, by Kate Chopin.

The story was interesting because it took place in Louisiana, in bayou country not so very far from Crowley. But it was also scandalous. It told the story of a woman who had everything a woman was supposed to want: a handsome, successful husband; children; a beautiful house.

But she was unhappy to be just a wife and mother, and she finally left her husband to live on her own. After a life spent "feeding on the opinion of others," she chose to be her own person.

The book had caused an uproar. Newspaper writers had denounced it for encouraging women to abandon their families. Rose thought it was beautifully written, and certain passages spoke right to her: "She began to look with her own eyes; to see and to apprehend the deeper undercurrents of life."

That was exactly what was happening to Rose. She was beginning to see the world with her own eyes, to make her own choices without trying to please her parents or worry so much about what other people expected of her.

Of course, Rose wanted to be a wife and mother. But this was a modern age. Any woman who really wished could be both an independent-minded person and raise a family. She was sure of it.

Her thoughts snagged on the hard sound

of E.J.'s raised voice floating in from the kitchen.

"WHAT!"

She set the book down and softly walked down the hall where she could hear better. The swinging door to the kitchen stood open. Viola was standing at the ironing board. E.J. stood over the table where she had been cutting up a pumpkin for pies.

"That's impossible, Viola," E.J. said, knife paused in midair. "No one can order you to leave town."

"Yes, Mrs. Thayer," Viola said, shaking her head. "Sheriff Sloane told me I have to be out of town by Monday morning."

E.J. set down her knife and wiped her hands on her apron.

"Viola, you sit right down now and tell me what this is all about."

E.J. spotted Rose in the doorway but didn't send her away. Rose was glad Wilder was off playing at a friend's house; otherwise, E.J. might have asked her to keep him busy. Whatever Viola had to say, it surely wasn't meant for the ears of a child.

Rose leaned against the doorjamb, her chest tightened with dread, and listened while Viola poured out her tale.

Viola had lately been working a second job, in the evenings, taking care of a sick woman, Mrs. McCarthy. E.J. had helped her get that job because Viola was trying to save up some money to help one of her brothers, who wanted to go to college. Viola had three other brothers and sisters, and every one was trying to save the money to help him.

Poor Mrs. McCarthy had been sick a long time, and had been bedridden almost a year. Mr. McCarthy was an important man in the parish. He had a real estate office on Parkerson Avenue. He also had a seat on the Acadia Parish Police Jury. That was the name of the group of men who governed the parish. They decided which roads to fix, made the laws, collected the taxes, and hired the sheriff. Police Jury was an odd name, but that was what they called it.

Poor old Mrs. McCarthy was dying, and

Viola had been helping to feed her, to keep her clean and comfortable. Mr. McCarthy had been very kind to Viola, giving her a ham from a hog he had slaughtered. He had been very friendly to her.

Then, one day, he said he was going to his sister's house in New Orleans for a week so he could attend to some out-of-town business, while his sister would come here to take care of his wife. He was going to stay in his sister's house and asked Viola to go with him, so she could do the housekeeping.

"I told him I couldn't do that," Viola said. "Why, I have you to think of, Mrs. Thayer. And it just wouldn't be right, traveling with a married man, just him and me."

"Certainly not," E.J. quickly agreed.

"But when I told him so, Mrs. Thayer, he just laughed it off."

E.J.'s eyes narrowed. She knew there was more to it than that.

"Last Thursday night, Mr. McCarthy asked me again." Viola stared at the tabletop and picked at a cuticle. She continued in a quiet voice. "He took up just begging me please to go to New Orleans with him, or who'd cook his supper and iron his shirts?

"I told him it wouldn't be right, with Mrs. McCarthy home sick as she is, poor thing. But he just kept asking, and then he started shoutin' at me."

"It's simply disgraceful!" E.J. exploded. She was like a cat leaping on its prey. "Bullying a poor child like that. I'd like to give him a piece of my mind."

"Mrs. Thayer, don't you, please!" Viola cried. "I got enough worriment without you getting your own self tangled in it. It's a real bad thing to get messed up in a nigra's troubles. You don't know, Mrs. Thayer. You're from up north."

E.J.'s eyes flashed.

Rose's stomach churned. Viola gave E.J. such a pitiful look that tears welled in her eyes.

"So I just ran out, Mrs. Thayer. I ran out and left my sweater right on the hall tree. And now Mr. McCarthy, he's gone and told the sheriff I stole his money. The sheriff came to the house and told my mammy and pappy I've got to leave town by Monday morning."

Viola shook her head. Even she had trouble believing what had happened. E.J.'s fists tightened into balls on the tabletop. Her cheeks flushed pink.

"Mrs. Thayer, I didn't steal any money," Viola pleaded, twisting her hands together. "Honest. I didn't take a thing. Now where'm I going to go? Where on God's earth am I going to go?" Viola buried her face in her hands and wept.

No one had to say it: Of course Viola hadn't stolen anything. She was as good as gold. Anyone could see it. She had worked for E.J. for more than a year, and E.J. would have trusted Viola with her life.

E.J. looked like a mule about to kick. If they could have, her ears would have been flat back. The veins stood out on her forehead. Her mouth was a tight line.

She rose slowly from the table, then paused

for a moment, looking down at Viola with fire crackling in her eyes.

Then she sighed heavily. The lines in her face softened. "I am going to think about this," she announced. "I am going to think about this, and, as God is my witness, Mr. McCarthy is not going to get away with it."

E.J. untied her apron. "Viola, get your things. I want you to go home and stay there 'til this business is settled. You understand?"

"Yes, ma'am," Viola said. "But Mrs. Thayer, you best not stir folks up. It's a bad, bad thing."

"I have lived a good half century and managed to survive it in spite of myself," E.J. said, hanging her apron on its hook on the door. "Don't you worry about me and don't you lose your hope."

She took Viola by the shoulders. Viola shook her head woefully. Her shoulders slumped. "You don't give up your faith, now," E.J. insisted. "There are plenty of decent-minded folks in this town, northerners and others who won't stand for such nonsense. You leave it to me."

Viola wiped away a tear. In a small voice she said, simply, "Yes, ma'am."

E.J. telephoned for a hack to come and take Viola home. When it got there, E.J. gave Viola her next week's wages. Viola tried to refuse, but E.J. said she might need it, and they would settle up later.

Then Viola was gone.

Rose could think of nothing to say. She followed E.J. as she marched heavy-footed down the hallway. The globe on the hall lamp rattled angrily as she passed.

"What will you do?" Rose finally asked.

E.J. strode to the telephone and cranked the handle with such fury it came out of its socket. She replaced the handle and jammed the receiver against her ear.

"Central?" she barked. "Get me Sheriff Sloane. . . . Never you mind what for. Just get him on the line. . . . Yes, I'll wait. And the rest of you can just hang up!"

E.J. wouldn't tell Sheriff Sloane what she wanted to talk to him about on the phone. Too many people were listening. She made an appointment to meet him the next day at the courthouse.

Rose stayed home. It poured on and off all day, so she couldn't go buggy riding with Mr. Skidmore. Even if the weather had been perfect, Rose wasn't in a sociable mood.

She would have gone to visit Viola, but E.J. wouldn't hear of it.

Rose argued, but E.J. said there were some people who might not understand. Rose didn't care, but E.J. continued, "Besides, Rose, it would embarrass Viola. Think what her family would feel, and what her neighbors would say. They'd all want to know what was going on. You don't want to do that, do you?"

Rose sighed. She hadn't thought about it that way.

She knew she couldn't go with E.J. to the sheriff's office. She didn't even want to. So she stayed behind and tried to study, but her mind kept straying from her work. She stared into space, thinking and wondering.

She bolted at the jingle of harness on a

passing team and hurried to look out the window. She paced the hallway, from the kitchen to the parlor.

When E.J. finally got home, she didn't have much to tell. Sheriff Sloane had said he had his orders, and until those orders changed, he was going to see Viola on the train tomorrow morning.

After supper Rose made a fresh pot of coffee. She went to her studies. Later, when she went to the kitchen to wash her cup, she noticed a light coming from the parlor door. She peeked around the corner. E.J. sat in her morris chair, wrapped in a shawl, reading her Bible.

"Get some rest," Rose said softly.

"Good night, Rose. I'll try."

But as Rose climbed into bed she knew E.J. would have no rest until she had done everything she could to get her way. E.J. lived with problems, and this one was big.

Bienvenue

The next morning Viola left Crowley on an eastbound local. She would stay with relations in Grand Coteau, a town about forty miles away. Rose insisted on missing school to go to the depot with E.J. to see her off. E.J. and Sheriff Sloane said hardly three words to each other as they stood on the depot platform.

E.J. gave Viola a box lunch and fussed over her like a mother hen. When the train came hissing and clanking into the depot, Sheriff Sloane reached to pick up Viola's bag, but E.J. grabbed it first. "I'll take that," she snapped.

They found the car that was for black people only and handed Viola's grip to the conductor.

Viola cried. Rose cried. E.J. wouldn't give Sheriff Sloane the pleasure. She waited until they were out of his sight.

E.J. still hadn't said what she was going to do about Viola, and her mood was grim all the rest of that day. When Wilder asked where Viola was, E.J. snapped at him, "She's gone to her relations. Now go tidy your room and be quick about it. I won't have this place becoming a pigsty."

In the next days Viola's mother, Maybelle Littleton, came by to help out with the chores.

Isaac still drove Rose to and from school, but she explained to him that Viola had taken ill and she must pitch in around the house. He was very polite about it, but Rose could see his feelings were hurt. She wanted to tell him what had happened, but E.J. had said not to let on to a soul. "The less folks know about it, the better."

Meanwhile, E.J. spent hours at her desk in the parlor, poring over books and pamphlets, and writing furiously. One day, when Rose and E.J. walked to Parkerson Avenue to order groceries, E.J. announced, "Let's pay Mr. McCarthy a visit." Just outside the door to his real estate office, E.J. paused and took a deep breath. Then she charged right in.

The bell jangled merrily as the door swung open. Rose stood just inside the door, biting her lip, as E.J. marched up to Mr. McCarthy's desk without so much as a hello. He looked up and smiled at first.

"Mrs. Thayer," he began. He hesitated, and a frown swept over his face.

Rose was surprised to see how harmless-looking he was, gray-haired, short, and squat.

"Mr. McCarthy, I thought you might take some benefit from the writings of a good and decent man." She handed him a pamphlet that Rose recognized: It was a printing of Abraham Lincoln's Emancipation Proclamation that the Social Democrats sometimes handed out. Then E.J. gave him a second pamphlet, one that she had gotten from church.

Mr. McCarthy stared at the pamphlets and then at E.J. His mouth worked, but nothing came out as E.J. wheeled and sailed back out of his office, with Rose trailing behind.

"He'll probably throw them in the trash, but I expect I gave him something to think about," E.J. explained with a mischievous chuckle. "Maybe he has not heard that slavery is ended."

After that, E.J. stopped in to Mr. McCarthy's office as often as she was downtown. She always left him some writings. She even went so far as to copy down some inspirational passages she found in books, and from the Bible.

"There are times for armed battle, and times that call for quiet prayer," E.J. said one day as she sat at her desk, flipping the pages of a book. "If I have learned anything about men it is that they can be led, but never driven."

Mr. McCarthy was always very polite with E.J. In his presence Viola's name never passed her lips, but E.J. said there was no doubt he understood why she had taken a sudden interest in saving his soul. She was sure his conscience was working on him. "Every man knows where his own shoe pinches," she said.

A week went by, but nothing changed. Rose began to think that Viola would never come back, no matter what E.J. did. It was as if the light had gone out of the house.

Maybelle was a great help to E.J., but Rose missed Viola's spirited voice. The whole business made her terribly sad, and angry. How could the world be so plainly unjust, and nothing to be done about it?

E.J. was sure of her methods, but Rose couldn't pass Mr. McCarthy's office without wanting to give him an unpleasant piece of her mind.

One day when Rose stopped at the bakery on her way home, Odile surprised her with an invitation.

"My family, I 'ave told many times about you. Now my papa and mama, they want to meet you. You must come to my 'ouse for a visit."

Rose was delighted, and they arranged for her to come home with Odile the next Saturday. She insisted that Rose stay the night. "Bring your Sunday dress," she said. "You must come with me to Mass. This Sunday, it is Advent. I think you will find it very interesting."

With her grip packed with her best dress and shoes, she met Odile at the bakery after dinner on Saturday. It was a clear day, cool and sunny after a hard rain.

Odile's father, Mr. Boudreaux, met them with his wagon, loaded with the week's trade: sacks of flour and rice, a large box of salt, and a bolt of muslin. Two of Odile's younger brothers, both beautiful little boys with great mops of hair, rode with him

Only Odile spoke English. "My father, he speaks only a little English and he is ashamed for the way he speaks it. In town some people make fun of him."

So speaking to Mr. Boudreaux and Odile's brothers was complicated by Odile's translations. Most of the time, Rose did not understand much of what was being said. Odile couldn't translate every word. But it didn't matter. Rose loved just hearing the sound of the language, and especially the laughter and banter among the Boudreaux.

Mr. Boudreaux seemed to laugh the most. He had the clearest blue eyes in a face deeply lined and tanned—the honest face of a farmer, Rose thought. He wore a great mustache, and when he spoke his eyebrows worked comically up and down. He waved his free hand, slapping his knee now and then for punctuation.

A pair of mules pulled the wagon through the gumbo mud. Rose felt herself being carried back to the days when she was a child, living on the farm with Mama and Papa. She remembered how thrilling it was to go into town on the wagon on Saturdays.

"Papa, he wants me to tell you the names of all the children," Odile said. "These two, they are Oliver and Octave." The little boys stopped wrestling for an instant at the sound of their names.

"At home there are Onesia, Ovide, Ophelia, Olivia, and Opta. My sisters Odalia, Odelia, and Olite, they are married. And also my brothers, Otta and Omea."

Rose burst out laughing. "How many is that?" she cried in amazement.

"We are thirteen," Odile said. "Two more, they died when they were born."

Odile had twelve brothers and sisters, and poor Mrs. Boudreaux had given birth to fifteen babies! Rose had always wished to be part of a large family, but she couldn't imagine giving birth to it.

The long ride took them deep into the back country some miles from Crowley. Along the way they passed the edges of several narrow bayous. At one of them Mr. Boudreaux pointed and said something. Odile and the boys jumped up to look. Rose craned to see.

It was an alligator, sunning itself on a little island. The alligator was enormous, scaly, with a long snout and a mouth that was set in a wicked, toothy grin.

The alligator lifted its gruesome head at the sound of the wagon. Then it pushed with its hind feet and slid its leathery hide down the mud embankment, grinning all the way. It disappeared under the darkly stained water like a sinking log. Only a faint ripple showed what direction it had headed.

Rose promised herself she would never, ever go swimming in a bayou.

Finally the wagon came to a clearing along one of the bayous. Rose could see the buildings of a small farm.

"*On arrive*," Odile said. "We are here."

The house did not look as large as Rose expected for a family of so many souls. But it had many additions built on to it. The barn and house and all the outbuildings were finished in unpainted planks.

Around the large barnyard there was a picket fence of rough-hewn boards. The barn was covered with the drying skins of muskrats. Rose had heard in town that the Acadians did a big trade in fur. Without trapping, Odile's family would starve, and the swamps were full of muskrats.

As they got closer Rose realized that the Boudreaux farm was on a peninsula right on the edge of the swamp. It was surrounded on three sides by water, like a cozy little island.

Several cows stood in the water, and a horse grazed along the bank. The water was so still and black that the cows and trees made a perfect reflection.

True to Odile's word, there were children of every age everywhere. A boy was chopping wood, a little girl swung on a rope from a chinaberry tree that had had all its branches hacked back.

An older girl came out of the house and threw a panful of wash water on the ground. On the bayou a young man was standing in a narrow, shallow boat, pushing himself forward with a long pole. The boat was shaped like half of a pea pod.

A column of smoke rose straight up into the air from a smokehouse, and from a chimney in the house. And from all the trees hung wisps of moss.

As she looked at that farm, heard the sounds of livestock and children, and smelled the manure and smoke, such a wistful feeling came over Rose. She had grown up on a farm, but as an only child. How often she had wanted to be part of a big, noisy family! This was almost like coming back to the home she'd always dreamed of but never had.

One by one the children ran over to the wagon, until a crowd had gathered. They were jumping up and down and talking and waving their arms.

"*Papa! Papa! Avez-vous quelque chose?*" "*Papa, lagniappe?*"

Everyone was talking at once. "The children, they want to know if Father has brought them a *lagniappe*, a gift, from town," Odile said, laughing.

Mr. Boudreaux had brought them all stick candy that he doled out from a paper sack. The children made humming noises as it disappeared into their mouths.

Bienvenue

Mrs. Boudreaux came out of the house, and Rose was introduced all around. She found herself laughing but not knowing what she was laughing at. All the names sounded alike. But they were all so friendly and cheerful, she was just glad to be among them.

Mrs. Boudreaux wore a scarf over her hair, and her eyes crinkled kindly as she shook Rose's hand. *"Bienvenue,"* she said, which Odile had taught her meant "welcome." In fact everyone shook her hand, even the littlest girl, who also wished her *"Bienvenue."* Rose was enchanted by how polite and warm they all were.

"Merci. Merci," Rose answered. It was all the French she could remember in all that noise and confusion.

Now that she was out in the country, Rose envied the girls and Mrs. Boudreaux in their simple everyday dresses.

"I feel so foolish in these city clothes," Rose said. "I don't know what I was thinking about when I dressed myself."

Mrs. Boudreaux looked at Odile with

165

questioning eyes. Odile repeated what Rose had said, in French. Mrs. Boudreaux said something, and Odile translated: "*Maman*, my mother, she says you and I, we are the same size. Why don't I lend you one of my everyday dresses? Do you want to do that?"

"Yes!" Rose said gratefully. "Yes, I would feel so much more comfortable. Thank you."

One of the boys carried Rose's grip into the house, and Odile showed Rose where they would sleep. The room was simple and rustic, and Rose loved it. Over the big double bed was a picture of Jesus, and there was a cross on the wall by the dresser.

There was no glass in the window, only shutters that could be pulled tight to keep out the cold. Rose was glad she had thought to bring a union suit. She wriggled out of her waist, corset, and skirt. Then she put on the union suit and pulled Odile's loose cotton dress over her head.

Rose sighed with relief. She almost wished she could take off her shoes, or at least had a pair of old brogans like the ones she used to wear as a child.

The last thing she did was to let down the braid she had tightly coiled at the back of her head. Now she really felt relaxed.

The first thing, Odile said, was to sit and have some coffee. "Coffee, it is the tradition," she said. "We drink it all the time, all day, and even in the night. Papa, he carries his coffee with him, in a flask."

Rose sat in the kitchen with Mr. and Mrs. Boudreaux and Odile. The other children popped in and out, pausing for a few moments to look at Rose with curious, wondering eyes and then running outside to play or tend to their chores.

Mrs. Boudreaux served the coffee in tiny little cups that looked almost like doll furniture. *"Tasses,"* Odile called them. They drank so many cups of coffee, this must be a way to save on the cost, Rose thought.

She was thirsty and took a big sip. Then she discovered the real reason for the little cups. Viola made strong coffee for E.J., but this was so potent it took Rose's breath away. She stared hard into the cup.

Everyone burst out laughing.

"Oh, I'm so sorry," Rose said, blushing. "I didn't mean to be rude. It's just that—"

"No, no," Odile said. "It amuses us, when the English drink our coffee for the first time. Take small sips, like this."

Sitting in that plain, cozy kitchen, listening to the Boudreaux family chatter in French, drinking the strong, muddy coffee out of a thimble-sized cup at the edge of a swamp full of alligators and goodness knew what else, Rose felt as far from home as she could be and still be on the Earth. Mansfield, Mama and Papa, her life in Missouri—she could hardly remember them anymore. Like a dream recalled upon waking, it seemed to be fading.

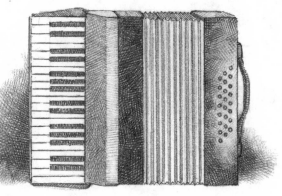

A Life Agreeable

Odile took Rose for a walk around the farm. The house faced the water, and went back for a distance, then formed a T. The many additions made it look as if it had been built by a man who often changed his mind. The house had grown as the children were born.

The kitchen was a separate room, connected to the rest of the house by a very short raised walk. It had its own doorway to the outdoors, and a wide chimney made of mud and moss. The whole house sat on cypress stumps. There were no big stones, and cypress grew right in the swamp. It wouldn't rot.

The only side of the house that had been painted was the front, where the gallery was. The wall was red, and the shutters, door, and gallery posts were green.

The front door swung out instead of in, the way doors did in every other house Rose had seen. When she looked inside, she saw why: there was no room for the door to swing. At the end of the gallery a set of outside stairs rose to the second floor where the boys and bachelor men slept.

Under the trees in the yard was a small squat mound of mud. It was rounded on top, built over a wooden base. That was the baking oven. "For making the breads," Odile said.

They were standing in the yard when Rose noticed Mrs. Boudreaux reach through an open window in the kitchen. She set a pot on a little wooden shelf attached to the side of the house at the sill. She reached out with a kettle, poured hot water in the pot, and began to scrub it. She scanned the barnyard as she did it, scolding one of the boys, who had been chasing a chicken.

How clever, Rose thought. Mrs. Boudreaux could wash her dishes without getting water on her floor, and she could keep track of her family at the same time.

Everything about the Boudreaux farm seemed to bring the indoors out, and the outdoors in. You could never do it in Missouri, where the winters were longer and colder. Here it was the end of November, and they had not even had a frost.

Rose pestered Odile with questions, and made her say and spell the French word for everything. "House" was *maison*. "Gallery" was *galerie*. "Dog" was *chien*. "Cat" was *chat*. "Tree" was *arbre*. So many French words made sense to Rose, and fit perfectly with her Latin grammar as well.

"Why is the chinaberry tree chopped off like that?" Rose wanted to know. The tree looked grotesque, with its thick trunk and branches hacked almost completely off.

"Papa, he does it every fall," Odile said. "To get the wood for cooking. It grows back in the spring, very fast."

Rose realized that in Missouri they depended on an endless supply of cheap wood for cooking and heating. There weren't many trees here, and coal was very expensive.

The little shell-shaped boat was called a *pirogue*. "The water is very shallow in some places, where Papa has his traps," Odile explained. "The pirogue, he says it can travel on a dew."

Mrs. Boudreaux had cooked a gumbo made of turtle meat. Odile called it terrapin stew. The whole family gathered together in the kitchen to eat: Oliver, Octave, Odile, Onesia, Ovide, Ophelia, Olivia, Opta, Rose, and Mr. and Mrs. Boudreaux. Just as they were about to sit down, one of Odile's older brothers came with his wife, and they joined in, too. There never was a merrier table.

The stew was dark, thick, and rich, with fine bits of turtle meat, onion, and peppers. They ate from bowls, using hunks of bread to wipe the dish dry of the gravy. Rose even had a small glass of wine with her supper.

She was surprised to find that she enjoyed it. It perfectly complemented the flavor of the stew.

There were always five different conversations going at the same time, and Odile could not eat and translate. Rose spent most of the meal listening and watching. She managed to compliment Mrs. Boudreaux on the delicious meal. *"Très bon,"* she said, and everyone laughed good-naturedly.

Mr. Boudreaux said something to Odile, and Odile said to Rose, "My father, he asks you how do you find our little-little life?"

"Tell him I was raised on a small farm myself, but I wish it had been like this, with many children and so much laughter."

Mr. and Mrs. Boudreaux nodded their heads knowingly, and the rest of the children stifled their squirming and chattering to listen. Mr. Boudreaux pulled his pipe from his pocket and filled it with tobacco.

"I think," Rose went on, "that you are very blessed to have such a beautiful family, and to live in such a beautiful place. It is an honest life."

Mr. Boudreaux nodded, lighting his pipe. He drew hard and let out a big puff of smoke. Then he spoke to Odile.

"My father, he asks you if you know the history of the Acadians?" Odile translated.

"Yes, a little," Rose answered.

Odile translated her father's story: "We are simple people," Mr. Boudreaux said. "Our families, they came from France to find peace and tranquillity. Then we suffered. Our families, they were torn apart, and finally we came to this place where there were only the Choctaw Indians. We lived in peace with them because we did not cheat them.

"Now, here, it is our promised land. We are a people of small men, who work at small occupations. Here, we have a life agreeable."

Everyone nodded. Rose thought there could be no more contented people than Odile's family. She so wished she could speak to them directly and understand every shade and meaning of their words and expressions.

A Life Agreeable

They were up very late that night. More of Odile's family came to visit, and one of the boys brought out an accordion. Fresh coffee was brewed. The boys moved the big table out of the kitchen, and they made a little frolic, right there in their own house.

"*Fais-dodo!*" one of the boys cried out, and everyone laughed.

"My brother, he says we are making a party, a *fais-dodo*," said Odile. "But truly it is not a *fais-dodo*. Everyone must come, all the family and all the neighbors. Everyone. Tonight we make a small one for ourselves."

"*Fais-dodo?*" Rose wondered. It was pronounced "fay dough-dough."

"It means, exactly, to make a sleep. When we make a party for dancing, we stay awake all the night. We make ourselves very tired, to go to sleep."

Even though it was just a *fais-dodo* for the family, some neighbors did show up. How they knew, Rose never understood. Every room in the house blazed with lamplight, and was filled with merriment.

Some of the older people played cards at a small table in the corner of the kitchen while the young people danced to lively accordion music. Rose had never heard such a spirited sound, more stirring and joyful even than the fiddle tunes that she knew from Missouri.

Everyone danced, at least a little. Odile taught Rose an Acadian step, and Rose taught her a reel. The house shook with stamping feet. Even the little ones joined in.

When they grew tired, they sat and talked. Soon Mr. Boudreaux was telling jokes and stories. All the family gathered around. More coffee was brewed and served in tasses. And Odile sat next to Rose, whispering in her ear the English translation:

"Old Mr. Richard, one day he goes out from the bayou into town for his trade. He goes to the store and asks the storekeeper, 'How are eggs?' The storekeeper says, 'Sir, the good ones, they are fifteen cents a dozen. The ones that are a little bit cracked, they are ten cents a dozen.'

"Mr. Richard, he thinks a minute and says,

'Okay. Crack me three dozen.'"

The room rang with laughter.

Mr. Boudreaux told tall tales, much like the tall tales Rose had heard in the Ozarks, but with a twist. A man caught a catfish that was six axe-handle lengths between its eyes. He had to build a pot big enough to cook it in, and the pot was so big, the man hammering on one side couldn't hear the hammering of the man on the other.

Rose volunteered to tell an Ozark story.

"Ouais, ouais!" everyone cried out—Yes, yes! Rose had noticed that the Acadians said *"oui"* to mean simple "yes," and *"ouais"* to say it informally. It sounded like the difference between "yes" and "yeah."

Rose told the tall tale about the Ozark pumpkins that grew so fast they got worn down to nothing from being dragged over the rocks. Then she told the one about the Ozark summer that was so hot the corn popped in the field and drifted against the fences so high the mules thought it was snow, caught cold, and nearly froze to death.

Finally, the neighbors drifted off. Then Odile's aunts and uncles and married sisters and brothers went home. The children who had fallen asleep here and there like discarded rag dolls were scooped up and tucked into their beds.

Rose and Odile were the last ones awake. "My mouth, it is tired, and my head hurts from thinking," Odile said. It *was* a relief to stop talking, trying to keep up with the conversation.

So they sat quietly out on the gallery, looking at the moonlit swamp, listening to the small sounds of the night creatures. An owl hooted somewhere far away. The dog barked once from his sleeping spot in the barn, then fell silent. A bird chirped in its sleep.

Rose had enjoyed moments like these at home on the farm. She always wanted them to go on forever.

The next morning Rose woke to the smell of strong coffee. Odile was already up and dressed, standing by the bed with a tray with two cups and some biscuits.

Rose rubbed her eyes and yawned. "Coffee in bed?"

"It is another tradition," Odile said.

Rose was shocked to discover it was already ten o'clock. She'd never slept so late. She had to hurry to dress in time for church.

Rose was sorry to leave the farm as Mr. Boudreaux drove the wagon away. They had put clean cloths in the wagon box so they could sit and not soil their clothing. Rose and the older children sat on one side, and all the little children were lined up like dolls in a row on the other.

Odile pointed to her littlest sister, all frilly with lace and ruffles, like a spring cabbage. She said to one of her brothers, *"N'est-ce pas qu'elle est une goélette bien grée?"* The little girl giggled and stuck her thumb in her mouth.

"It is an expression," Odile said. "She looks like a fine little boat, all rigged out."

They drove into Crowley, to the Catholic church. Rose watched awkwardly as each member of the family dipped the fingers of one hand into a bowl of holy water at the entrance, then knelt and made the sign of the cross. Rose didn't know what to do with herself, and she almost fell over when she started to kneel and then decided not to. But no one scowled. They seemed to understand, and Rose even noticed a few smiles.

She enjoyed the pageantry of the Mass, the long robes of the priests, the violet four-cornered cap that the priest wore. At one point he lit a sweet-smelling substance in a metal ball. Then he swung it back and forth, sending the fragrant smoke drifting over the congregation and making columns of light in the sun rays.

The whole service was in Latin. Rose understood almost all of it, and marveled at how beautifully the priest spoke the words. He made them into a mournful chant that seemed to hover in the air, and rise to the heavens.

"In nomine Patris, et Filii, et Spiritus Sancti, Amen."

They all crossed themselves one more time, and then Rose's visit was over. Outside the church Rose told Odile that she would walk herself home, but Mr. Boudreaux insisted on driving. After all, she had a bag to carry, and the streets were still very muddy.

She hadn't wanted the family to see where she lived, to see E.J.'s enormous house and get the idea that Rose was not like them. She felt guilty. But when she climbed down from the wagon, none of them showed her anything but warmth and good cheer.

"Good-bye, Rose," Odile said. *"Au revoir! Adieu!"* everyone shouted. They all waved. The wagon looked so happy and festive, they could have been in a parade.

"À bientôt!" Rose called out as they drove off. "See you soon."

Meeting Mr. Debs

Rose turned seventeen on December 5. Mr. Skidmore took her for supper to a restaurant, and gave her a beautiful silver-and-tortoiseshell hair comb. Mama sent Rose a pair of new mittens and a brooch made of jet that had belonged to Grandma Ingalls. She put a note in the package:

Dearest Rose,
  We miss you most on this precious day. Have a wonderful birthday. Papa sends his love. You could write now and then.

Rose winced. She had written Mama and Papa only three letters and Paul only two.

As if he had read her mind, a package came from Paul the next day: a box of good chocolates, "because I hardly know anymore what it is you like, and you are the sweetest girl in the world. Please write, dear friend. June seems so far away."

Rose winced again. She must be more attentive to Paul or he would think she was losing interest. She promised herself she would find something special for him for Christmas, and include a long, newsy letter.

It wasn't that she didn't miss everyone. She was simply too busy to think about them much. She was having too good a time to brood or pine. She was selfish. She knew it. But there was nothing to be done about it.

Just before Christmas, Rose came home for dinner to find E.J. strutting about the house as proud as a rooster, puffed up and crowing.

"Rose, I have just now come back from

collecting Viola at the depot and taking her home!"

Rose whooped. "For good?"

"Yes. That rascal McCarthy told the sheriff he had decided not to press the issue any longer, seeing as how it was almost Christmas and all. An act of generosity in light of the season. Hmph!" E.J. huffed in disgust. "It just proves again that persistence is the greatest virtue."

Rose was elated. She knew her aunt could be cantankerous, and she did have a knack for putting her nose in places where it wasn't invited. But she held her beliefs like iron. Rose so admired her.

E.J. was also wise about people. "Remember this, Rose," she said. "Men are children, and they come in two varieties. One is gentle and sweet. The other is possessed of dull-witted, masculine vanity and think they were born to rule the world and everyone in it."

Rose thought about the men she knew. She decided E.J. was right, if you looked at it in a certain way. Rose took some comfort in

knowing that the men who were in her life—
Papa, Paul, Isaac—were sweet and gentle, not
the other kind.

All fall Rose had gotten perfect marks on
nearly every one of her Latin examinations.
Even in the two that she missed a perfect
mark, she had gotten only one or two small
things wrong.

She was so far ahead of the other scholars
in her Latin marks that unless she suddenly
fell behind, she knew she would be valedictorian. She had done well in her other subjects too, although algebra had given her
some difficulty.

Rose passed a comforting but humdrum
Christmas with Perley's family and Grandmother Wilder out on Perley's farm. Then
New Year's came, and it was 1904. The time
had flown since she arrived, and now it
seemed to go even faster.

She visited with Odile's family over another
Saturday night. This time she went with
Odile to a real *fais-dodo* and had a wonderful

time. She danced with several boys, and by the time she and Odile collapsed into bed, the sky had turned gray and the birds were singing.

Mr. Skidmore continued to court Rose, but she could tell he was beginning to lose interest. It wasn't anything particular that she noticed. Something was going unsaid between them. She guessed what they both were thinking: In a few short months they would be going back to their homes. There never had been and wouldn't be a future for their friendship. Rose thought maybe he even had a lady friend waiting for him in Chicago, the way Paul was waiting for her. She hoped so.

In January, E.J. received some wonderful news. Mr. Debs had agreed to visit Baton Rouge, the state capital, to make a public speech. That was excitement enough. But also he was personally going to give E.J. a gold watch to thank her for all the hard work she had done for the Social Democratic Party.

E.J. did the closest thing to a jig that

she could manage. She immediately sat down with the latest numbers of *Woman's Home Companion* and *The Ladies' World*, looking for a pattern for a new dress.

"'Tucks and shirrings continue to make the conspicuous features,'" E.J. read aloud to Rose one day as they sat in the parlor. "It also says here that white takes precedence of all colors. Imagine that! Why, I wouldn't have dreamed of wearing so much white in the old days. It just wasn't practical."

E.J. looked over her spectacles at Rose. "I suppose it's time I gave up my widow's weeds. What do you think?"

"I think you should meet Mr. Debs in a man's suit. He wouldn't ever forget you if you did it."

E.J. chuckled. "I might end up in jail, too. No, I'm too old to make a statement. Let me see, it should be warm by then. I'll make it up from a handkerchief lawn, with shoulder capes out of lace. Look at this fancy waist here, Rose. Do you think it would be too youthful on me?"

When she wasn't working on the dress, E.J. threw herself into persuading people to go to Baton Rouge. Everywhere she went, even if she had simply gone to the store to buy coffee, E.J. tried to drum up interest, among men as well as women.

"Maybe you don't agree with everything in the Social Democratic platform," E.J. told a blank-faced boy clerking at the Racket Store. She'd gone with Rose to buy thread, and the poor boy blinked dully as E.J. gave her little speech. "Maybe you don't even like Mr. Debs, although you would if you'd read this pamphlet and study his views. But he is a great speaker, and the causes he fights for are worthy and noble."

She handed out stacks and stacks of dodgers, and Rose helped when she could.

E.J. and some others talked the railroad into running an excursion train, just for people going to hear Mr. Debs. The trip was about an hour each way, so they could leave in the morning and be back the same day.

The excitement in E.J.'s house grew and

grew until finally the day came when Rose, E.J., Wilder, and dozens of other people from Crowley met at the depot to take the train to Baton Rouge. Gray skies and the threat of rain couldn't dampen their spirits. The cars already had a smattering of riders from towns to the west. When they reached Lafayette, the train became terribly crowded. But everyone was in a holiday mood.

To railroad men, Eugene V. Debs was a messiah. He had been a fireman on a locomotive when he was a boy, and had worked tirelessly for the railroad workers and led the American Railway Union through a bitter, violent strike. Railroad men just plain adored him.

Up and down the aisles there were hearty greetings, cordial introductions, long conversations about past experiences and future plans, exchanges of lunch box contents, card games, community singing, and even prayer meetings.

By the time the train pulled into Baton Rouge, everyone knew everyone else's name and as much of any person's background as they could tell. The lunch boxes were empty and their remains littered the seats and bare floors. The air smelled of grease and stale tobacco juice. The water cooler was empty, the dispenser out of paper cups. Thirsty children pleaded with helpless parents.

E.J., holding Wilder's hand tightly, stepped off the train. From the steps of the car Rose looked out over a sea of hats and feathers. Then she plunged into it, following E.J. as the crowd shuffled down the streets toward the capitol building. A light mist fell, but the air was mild with spring. No one even seemed to notice the rain.

E.J. parked Rose and Wilder under a tree on the capitol lawn while she went to find out where she was to meet Mr. Debs. They waited a long time. Rose entertained herself watching people, when she wasn't scolding Wilder not to climb the tree, or telling him to stop scuffing up his good shoes.

The size of the crowd overwhelmed her. Everyone was in a cheerful mood, but she had never been among so many people. Some women wore banners across their dresses that said VOTES FOR WOMEN. There were placards everywhere with sayings on them: MAN MAKES THE NATION, BUT WOMAN MAKES THE HOME. WORKERS OF THE WORLD UNITE.

Newsboys and hawkers drifted through the crowd selling newspapers, magazines, little American flags, fruit, candy, and soda pop. Rose was terribly thirsty, so she bought a five-cent bottle of Coca-Cola. It was her first taste of soda pop, and it was delicious. She shared it with Wilder.

The capitol rose majestically above them all. A broad marble stairway came down the front. A stage was set up there where Mr. Debs would speak.

Rose was beginning to get really worried, when E.J.'s face finally came bobbing toward her through the crowd.

"Come along," E.J. said quickly. "We haven't much time. He's *here*!"

Rose grabbed her skirts and hurried after E.J. and Wilder. They had to fight their way through the throng, then across the street into a large hotel. Inside, the hotel lobby was quiet as a church compared with the noise on the lawn. E.J. rounded a corner and marched over to where several men and two women were sitting in a group of stuffed chairs. They all rose at the sight of E.J.

One of the men was very tall, thin, and bald. A shorter man next to him whispered in his ear. The tall man smiled at E.J. and put out his hand to shake hers.

"Well, Mrs. Thayer. It's quite a crowd out there, isn't it?"

E.J. dabbed at her brow with her handkerchief, trying to catch her breath.

"Please," said Mr. Debs. "Won't you sit for a moment?"

"Thank you." E.J. sat down in a chair right next to him. "This is my niece, Miss Rose Wilder, and my son, Wilder Thayer."

Rose stared, stupefied. Her senses deserted her. It had all happened so fast, and now it hit her so hard she was light-headed. Eugene V. Debs was looking at *her*, and suddenly she was shaking his bony hand.

After that Rose had no notion what E.J. was saying or what Mr. Debs said back to her. She saw Mr. Debs hand E.J. an opened jewelry box with the gold watch in it. E.J. thanked him, shaking his hand, and then they were walking out of the hotel.

"Oh, E.J.!" Rose finally managed to cry out. "It was really him, wasn't it?"

E.J. stopped on the sidewalk but she didn't answer or turn around. Rose went to her and was shocked to see tears in her eyes. Rose stood close, saying nothing.

E.J. got her composure back, and dried her eyes. "There he was," she said in wonderment. "Gene Debs, the living link between God and man." That was all she said about it.

"All right, now. Let's find ourselves a good place to see and hear him."

E.J. led them all again, dragging Wilder, who was cranky and fussing. They found an open spot next to a fountain. As soon as they got there, a shout swept through the crowd, again and again. Rose couldn't tell what they were saying at first. But then it was unmistakable: "DEBS! DEBS! DEBS! DEBS!"

Everyone stirred with anticipation. Heads whirled this way and that, trying to catch a first glimpse. Then, he was there, on the stage, the same tall man, but the distance made him look even thinner, and more frail.

He leaned out with both arms raised, smiling over the roaring crowd. Women were crying; men shouted themselves hoarse. Rose felt it herself. She was not going to cry, or even to shout. But a wild feeling blew up inside of her, a kind of love she had never experienced. It was as if the crowd were one great person, hugging the tall, frail man on the stage.

The crowd roared and roared, as if it would never stop. Mr. Debs stood on the platform, letting the people love him. Then, slowly, the noise began to fade. A stillness gathered, like the hush that comes with a gentle, heavy snow.

Now the only voice was his. It was a voice that could do with the crowd what it willed,

Rose thought, because of the great warm heart that everyone felt speaking there. Rose listened, tingling all over.

She couldn't hear very well at first, and then his words came clearly across the multitude of heads in front of her.

"The capitalist refers to you as mill hands, farm hands, factory hands, machine hands. Hands, hands!" he cried in a voice filled with outrage. He paused and let the word echo in the silence. Somewhere a woman screamed.

"A capitalist would feel insulted if you called him a hand. Because he's a head." He paused again.

"The trouble is, he owns *his* head and *your* hands!"

The audience exploded and roared for a long time. Mr. Debs waited until they fell silent again.

"The rulers have always ground the workingman beneath an iron heel. Crucifixion has always been the reward of men who are generous and see a higher vision. He who has dared to voice the protest of the oppressed and downtrodden has had to pay the penalty, all the way from Jesus Christ to Abraham Lincoln."

The crowd cheered. Handkerchiefs, including E.J.'s, were out all around Rose.

"But one day, when we are in partnership with the Goulds and the Rockefellers, the emperors of commerce, and have stopped clutching each other's throats—when we have stopped enslaving each other, we will stand together, hands clasped, and be comrades. We will be brothers. We will begin the march to the grandest civilization the human race has ever known!"

The crowd exploded again.

Mr. Debs spoke on, about votes for women, about public ownership of all essential industries. He said the Social Democratic Party stood for the sale of public land to small farmers, shorter work hours, and government pensions for old folks.

Then he began to speak about the Negro. Rose listened eagerly, wondering what Mr. Debs would say.

"The other day I was carrying two heavy grips away from the depot in a small southern town. I passed a group of local loafers sitting along a rail fence.

"A voice from the fence said, 'There's a nigra over there that'll carry your grips.' He pointed across the street at a Negro."

Mr. Debs pointed a bony finger toward the crowd. He began pacing back and forth on the platform.

"A second fence-sitter observed, 'That's what he's here for.' Then a third added, 'That's right, by God.'"

Mr. Debs paused and scowled, as if challenging the crowd.

"Ladies and gentlemen, those men were ignorant, lazy, unclean, void of ambition, themselves the foul products of the capitalistic system—held in the lowest contempt by the master class.

"Yet they raised themselves in their own esteem above the cleanest, most intelligent, and self-respecting Negro.

"We socialists have nothing special to offer

the Negro. We cannot make separate appeals to each of the races, because the Socialist Party is the party of the whole working class, regardless of color. But heed my words, comrades—white workers will never be free so long as Negroes are oppressed."

The crowd applauded, but held back its enthusiasm. Rose sensed that many of the people weren't sure they agreed with him. She worried that Mr. Debs had lost the audience. But a minute later he said something else that was marvelous and uplifting and they were cheering again. And then he was gone.

Rose stared out the window as the excursion train rattled its way back to Crowley. E.J. fell into a fitful sleep. Her weary head nodded and then fell against Rose's shoulder. Wilder lay sprawled across their laps, snoring. Rose was too exhausted to think, and too tired to care that the car smelled. It hadn't been cleaned while they were listening to Mr. Debs.

The only thing the passengers cared about now was getting home. Everyone was spent and rumpled.

At Lafayette half the people got off with sleepy good-byes to newly made friends. Rose woke Wilder and made him lie down on the empty seat across from her and E.J.

Her mind was a jumble of images and feelings and ideas. She knew this much: After this day, she would never be the same. She was a socialist now. She just didn't know what she would do about it.

Mardi Gras

In the middle of February, Odile invited Rose again to her house. This time she said it was for a very special occasion: Shrove Tuesday, Mardi Gras.

"What does it mean?" Rose asked.

"It means, exactly, 'Fat Tuesday,'" said Odile. "It is the last day before the beginning of Lent, the day before Ash Wednesday." On Ash Wednesday, she explained, every Catholic went to church. The priest smeared a bit of ash on each person's forehead. The ash was to remind people of the ashes from which they came and, when they die, to which they return.

Ash Wednesday was the beginning of Lent, which was forty days of penitence and abstinence from earthly pleasures that ended with the celebration of Christ's resurrection at Easter.

"The day before Lent begins, it is a big, big party. We eat hearty, make a big noise, and have a big, big *fais-dodo*."

On Monday night Rose rode home with Odile in her father's wagon. On Tuesday morning, after coffee in bed, everyone was up early. The little children were all stirred up, laughing, shouting, and running to the windows every minute to look out. Each one clutched a shiny new nickel.

Odile had said that some men would come to visit the house, "something like Santa Claus, but very different. It is the running of the Mardi Gras. *Le courir du Mardi Gras*."

Rose wanted to know more, but Odile said she didn't want to spoil the surprise of it.

Finally, one of the children let out a shriek that sounded like complete terror. Everyone ran outside, and there, down the lane, was a group of riders on horseback. Even from far away Rose could see there was something very odd about the riders. They were dressed in costumes, with strange hats.

One of the riders came trotting up to the fence. He wore a purple cape lined with gold-colored cloth, and a wide-brimmed hat with a long purple feather sticking out of it, and he carried a white flag.

But the strangest thing of all was his face, which was covered by a mask painted in many colors, with exaggerated features. The eyes had green circles around them, the large mouth was bright red, and there were yellow stripes on the white cheeks.

If she had run into someone like that on her own, Rose would have been scared out of her wits. He was dressed like something from a fantastic dream. But his bearing was regal. He dismounted, tied his horse to the fence, and let himself in through the gate.

All the Boudreaux were outside now, and one of the little girls clutched Mrs. Boudreaux's skirt, crying. The boys gawked at the rider with dinner-plate eyes.

He took off his hat with a great flourish, bowed, and said in a booming deep voice, *"Bonjour, la famille Boudreaux."* There was giggling all around. *"Vous voulez recevoir le Mardi Gras?"*

"What'd he say?" Rose whispered to Odile.

"He asks if we will receive the Mardi Gras."

"Oui, M'sieu le Capitaine! Allez-y!" Mr. Boudreaux shouted.

The man pulled a cow horn from under his cape, lifted his mask enough to put it to his lips, and blew a long note. Then he waved the flag. Instantly the crowd of riders came thundering down the lane at a full gallop, elbows and costumes flying. They came to a mud-spattering halt. They all began to dismount and tie up their horses.

The barnyard was suddenly full of costumed men in every possible kind of homemade clown attire. The little children screamed, and the grown-ups roared. Rose couldn't imagine what would happen next.

Some of the riders wore cloaks in bold stripes and dots. Some were brightly colored with fringe. Everyone wore pants of a different outlandish hue.

One very fat man was wearing potato sacks on all his limbs. Another wore a set of green curtains that had been sewn together around the neck. Others were dressed in women's clothing, with wigs and bustles. Rose guffawed.

They all wore masks, like the first rider, and funny peaked hats, some like dunce caps. But these hats were huge, in garish colors, and tilting crazily to the side.

An accordion and a fiddle appeared, and the men all began to dance and carry on like a clutch of monkeys. One of them rushed a little boy, swept him up in his arms, and tossed him, screaming with pleasure, into the arms of another man.

Another grabbed Mrs. Boudreaux and began to swing her around in a crazy dance. A man in a woman's dress, carrying a tiny parasol and a doll, tried to kiss Mr. Boudreaux.

Odile doubled over with laughter, then found herself snatched by one of the Mardi Gras men, who swung her around in a stumbling waltz.

Rose was next. This man wore a half mask that was blue with a long grotesque orange nose, and an orange wig sticking out from under a striped hat. He lifted her up, threw her over his shoulder, and started to carry her to his horse.

Rose screeched and kicked, laughing so hard she couldn't speak. The captain of the Mardi Gras came rushing over and pretended to whip the man who was carrying her. He quickly put her down and dashed around the house, the captain chasing him with the whip.

The man in the curtains squatted down and waddled like a duck up to the little girl holding Mrs. Boudreaux's skirt.

He held his hand out, palm up, and pointed with a finger on his other hand. *"Cinq sous!"* he begged in a squeaky voice. *"Cinq sous!"* ("Five cents!")

The little girl looked up uncertainly at Mrs. Boudreaux. Her mother whispered to her, and the little girl put her nickel in the man's hand.

Then he stood and bowed low. *"Merci,"* he said. *"Merci, Ti-Ti!"* ("Thank you, little one.")

The men went around begging from everyone in silly voices, and collecting nickels. Odile said you weren't supposed to know who the men were, and it was a game to guess if one of them might be a relative or friend or beau. They begged everyone for nickels, and then they asked for *poulets*—chickens.

Mr. Boudreaux brought out their two fattest hens, but it was up to the Mardi Gras riders to catch them, which made for more nonsense to laugh at. The chickens took off into the underbrush, followed by flapping clowns. The children laughed until their cheeks were wet with tears.

Finally the captain blew his horn again.

The chickens were caught and stuffed, squawking, into a sack. As the clowns mounted their horses, the captain invited the family to the *fais-dodo* to dance and "*manger le gros gumbo*," to eat a huge gumbo. Then the riders thundered off down the lane to the next house.

"Phew!" Rose said when the sound of pounding horse hooves had faded away.

In the afternoon Rose went with Odile and Mrs. Boudreaux to the house of a neighbor where there was a large barn. This was where the *fais-dodo* would be held. The women all helped prepare the meal, cooking the chickens that the riders had collected in the morning.

Iron wash pots were set out under the trees, fires were built under them, and the big gumbo was started.

The preparations went on for hours, with salting, tasting, and scolding when feathers were found in the thick soup. When the gumbo was done, the women went back to their homes to dress.

That night's *fais-dodo* was enormous and very rowdy. The barn thundered with dancing feet and thumping music. Outside in the night, there were several fights among the boys, and one of them had to be driven to the doctor for a knife wound. Rose saw none of that, but Odile said everyone was talking about it.

"Sometimes one boy, he gets very jealous if another boy, he dances with his girlfriend," Odile explained.

"We have the same problem in Missouri," Rose said. "Some of the country boys get stirred up at dances."

They watched the dancing for a few moments. Then Rose asked, "Odile, do you have a beau?" It was a question Rose had wanted to ask her many times, but she had been too shy.

Odile rolled her eyes. "*Mon Dieu!* My God! You have no idea how difficult it is," she said. "There is a song about it. In English it says,

"Go to sleep, my little one
Until the years to fifteen run.
When the fifteen years have fled,
Then my kitten will be wed."

Rose's eyebrows flew up. "You mean you are expected to marry at fifteen?"

Odile blew out her cheeks. "Yes, and no. My *grandmère*, she was married when she was thirteen and she was made a grandmother before she was thirty years.

"My mother, my sisters who are married, they are talking, talking to me about getting married. 'Odile, you know you like so-and-so,' they tease. 'Everybody knows you and him are going to make a marriage sometime, yes.'

"A girl, if she takes a beau, she is for certain going to marry him or there is trouble. No beau is better for me now."

Rose shook her head in disbelief. Married at thirteen. Why, Rose didn't know anything when she was thirteen! "In my family, I am not *expected* to marry anyone. But, of course,

I want to," she added quickly.

"That is good for you, Rose. A girl doesn't have a mind of her own around here. Everybody makes it up for you. They think a bad marriage is better than none."

Rose thought of Paul. He was the only boy she had ever thought of marrying. She knew they would marry one day. She also knew there were bad marriages.

But how could a girl know before she married a man whether it would be good or not? She felt a moment of doubt, then shook it off. Surely, she thought, I will know. I *must* know.

Femina Facit Domum

Spring was in full bloom on the Louisiana prairie before Papa would have even started his plowing back in Missouri. In March the bayous brimmed with rust-colored water as the snows of the north country began to melt and rush south along the Mississippi.

The ducks and geese that had spent the winter in the marshes left, and clouds of grackles arrived, spending their days wheeling and chattering over the courthouse. Songbirds appeared in twos on the telephone and electric wires. One day Rose even spotted a hummingbird, drawn to the bright-red paint on a farmer's wagon.

In the gardens peas bloomed, cabbage heads began to set, and patches of mustard greens were already topped with yellow flowers. In the early mornings, baby rabbits grazed alongside their mothers in Levy Park across the street.

Out on the farms sugarcane pushed up like sprouting corn, and rice farmers had already put their fields to seed. Soon, when the rice had sprouted and grown some, they would flood the diked fields with water pumped up from the bayous.

Growing inside of Rose was both excitement and dread. School would be ending soon, and then—what? She knew she would be going home. But she could not see any further into her future.

By April she was hardly seeing Mr. Skidmore anymore. She had decided to concentrate on her studies and had lost her interest in him anyway. One day he announced that he was returning to Chicago, and then he was gone.

When she wasn't at her studies, she was helping E.J. with her work for the Social Democrats and Mr. Debs's coming campaign for president. There were long, tiring meetings, and letter writing, and passing out dodgers.

None of this held Rose's attention. The one thing she kept thinking about was the valedictory speech. Professor Stover had all but said she would have that honor. She had caught all the way up to the other students in Latin, and earned near-perfect marks all the way along.

Now she was coming up with a plan to use her speech to talk about the things that truly mattered to her: socialism for the working-man, suffrage for women, and equality for all people. She talked about it one day with E.J. on the side gallery. They drank coffee that Rose had made in the French way, as Odile had taught her. E.J. was crocheting a baby's blanket for Perley and Elsie, who were expecting again.

It was a beautiful warm Saturday afternoon in May. The vines were fully leafed out and rustled gently in the breeze. A wren warbled nearby, and the high, light voices of children playing came from the park.

Rose told E.J. her plan.

"I think that is a perfect idea," E.J. said. "You can borrow a little bit here and there from Mr. Debs's speeches and writings. I think it would have a big effect. After all, this is the first class to graduate from our new high school. I'm sure all the Police Jury and the school board will be there, not to mention the parents of all the younger children."

Rose hadn't thought about that. She wondered if she had the courage to speak before so large a crowd, and so many important people.

"Don't you worry, Rose," said E.J., looking at her over the rims of her glasses. "If they have any brains at all, it'll give them something to chew on. If they don't, they won't understand a word."

But Rose wasn't as sure of herself as E.J. She remembered clearly the tension that came into the audience when Mr. Debs spoke on the Negro question in Baton Rouge. She decided she would ask Professor Stover.

All the students had begun preparing their presentations and orations for graduation day. Phala Baur would speak of the womanliness of Queen Victoria. Richard Schultz would speak about the English poet Lord Byron and his love for the Greek character. Mary Holt planned a piano recital.

Rose couldn't play the piano. She couldn't sing, and she didn't care to give a stuffy talk. She was rummaging through the books in the school library when she stumbled on a volume of Edgar Allan Poe. The first word that popped into her mind was "nevermore," from "The Raven."

She had always loved that poem. She thumbed the pages until she found it. Then she had an inspiration. She would borrow

Poe's poem and make it fit her class. Each stanza would end with the phrase "They would study, nevermore!" It would be a humorous way to say good-bye.

She thought it was terribly clever, and that night she wrote the whole thing out in an hour. She used everyone's name, and included a little humorous fact or two about each one. She hadn't spoken to Professor Stover yet.

One day the superintendent of the school came to visit. Professor Stover introduced him to each member of the class. Mr. Munson was a large man with bristling eyebrows and a mouth set in a grim line. Rose thought he must have been a very strict teacher.

"Mr. Munson is here today to see how we are all doing," Professor Stover said brightly. "Perhaps you would like to tell him something about our plans for the graduation ceremony."

Each of them described their orations or the performance they planned. When it was Rose's turn, she said she would give her own version of "The Raven." Mr. Munson seemed pleased. "I like that," he said loudly. "I like that very much: 'They would study, nevermore.' Very smart, and everyone will be able to grasp the humor of it."

Mr. Munson asked Professor Stover, "And who is our top Latin scholar, I wonder? Who will be the valedictorian?"

"That would be Miss Wilder," Professor Stover said. He told Mr. Munson how Rose had come all the way from Missouri knowing no Latin, and had managed to earn the best marks in the class.

"Splendid. Splendid! And what wisdom, may I ask, do you intend to impart from this lofty position?"

Rose gulped. Mr. Munson stood over her, thumbs in his vest pockets, an expectant smile on his face.

"Well," Rose began slowly, "I thought to speak on the question of . . . of women getting the vote." She didn't dare mention Mr. Debs's discussion of blacks.

A shadow passed over Mr. Munson's face. His smile crumpled into a frown, and he rubbed his hand over his mouth. He glanced at Professor Stover with raised eyebrows. Professor Stover just shrugged.

The room seemed deathly still as Rose waited for Mr. Munson to speak.

"Now," he finally said, "why would you want to stir folks up with a topic such as that?"

Rose started to feel queasy.

"It is an important question of the day," she said in a small voice. "I think people would like to hear something about women's suffrage."

Mr. Munson's face went dark.

"Woman suffrage!" He let forth the words like an explosion. "I don't like it, Miss Wilder. I don't like it a bit. I should think a bright young girl such as yourself would want to enlighten us about some aspect of ancient history, or speak hopefully of the future. You propose a tearing down of the family, throwing our traditions out the window."

Rose felt her dander getting up. She fought to control it.

"I *am* hopeful for the future, sir," she said. "I am hopeful that someday women will be the equal of men in law, as they are in fact. I am also hopeful that—"

"Now see here," Mr. Munson sputtered. His eyebrows met in the furrow of his frown. "I don't approve of votes for women, and neither does Mrs. Munson, I might add. Now *there's* a woman who doesn't care to hear what you think.

"But even if I did approve, I have no right to let such a controversial subject be presented on the platform of our graduation ceremony. This is a decent law-abiding town of citizens who just want to see their children dressed up and celebrating their educational achievements."

Rose felt the anger in his words like a hand pushing her lower into her chair. But she wouldn't be bullied.

"You teach us to think," she said defiantly. "But you don't want us to use our minds. Where is the sense in that?"

"That is just about enough, young lady.

There is no point in arguing the subject."

He waved his hand, as if brushing away a gnat. He turned to Professor Stover, who had backed away to stand against the wall. Rose saw that he would be no help to her at all.

"You see to it, Stover, that none of this clap-trap ends up in our graduation exercise," Mr. Munson ordered. "I want this to be a digni-fied affair. This is the last word I expect to hear on the subject."

"Yes sir," said Professor Stover.

Mr. Munson stormed out of the room.

Rose stared at her desktop for a long quiet moment, avoiding the embarrassed look she knew was on everyone's face. Then she gath-ered up her books, and, without a word, sailed out of Professor Stover's office.

"You must go back, Rose," E.J. said when Rose came stomping into the kitchen to tell what had happened. She was still trembling with rage.

"Oh, the stupid, stupid . . ." Then she collapsed into one of the kitchen chairs. "What can I do?" she wailed. "He won't let

me say what I believe. I can't just go ahead
and do it against his wishes. He might take
away my diploma!"

"He won't take away your diploma," E.J.
assured her. But Rose wasn't convinced, and
in any case she wouldn't do something so
deliberately contrary. Suppose she did, and
Mr. Munson wrote to Mama about it? No, she
was stuck, and hated it.

The next day Rose went back to class and
talked to Professor Stover.

"You will have to find a topic on your own,"
he said. "But I think you should keep it opti-
mistic, or something classical, perhaps. You
could write something in Latin."

Rose worried the thing to death. There was
no room in her mind for another thought. It
was so unfair!

She was sitting at the kitchen table one
evening after supper, doodling in her tablet.
She wrote: *Homo facit patriam, femina facit
domum.* Man makes the nation, woman makes
the home. She chewed on her pencil, thinking.

She liked the way that statement sounded in Latin. What could rhyme with "home"? she thought. Rome, dome, tome, foam.

Then she wrote: "That's the message of this little poem."

She began scribbling madly, one line in Latin, then a second line in English. Each line in Latin was a slogan or phrase about justice, and each line in English was innocent of any political ideas.

Without consciously thinking about it, Rose had solved her problem! She would recite a poem that spoke of her true feelings in words only her classmates and a few others could understand, and a poem of innocent fun that everyone else could enjoy.

She banged the table with her palm in triumph. "That's IT!" she cried out.

She rushed into the parlor and read the poem to E.J. She had to translate the Latin so E.J. could understand the joke, which made it sound clumsy. But E.J. clapped her hands with delight.

"Very good, Rose! I can't wait to see the

looks on some people's faces when they hear it. Does Munson know Latin?"

Rose wasn't sure, but they decided that even if he had studied it as a boy, he'd probably forgotten most of his vocabulary. And if by some chance he understood it perfectly, Mr. Munson would be a bigger fool to draw attention to the poem's true meaning by criticizing it.

It was brilliant, and Rose allowed herself to bask in her genius. She would have the last word after all.

Graduation Day

Now Rose began putting the finishing touches on her graduation dress. She and E.J. sewed together every night for nearly a week, switching to the oil lamp when the electricity went off.

The dress was all in white lawn, with yards and yards of snowy white lace and ruffles, and shirring around the hem, and a long shoulder cape. She chose a low collar, to show off her neck and to keep cool.

Then she experimented with her hair. Styles were changing so fast. She ended up piling it into a pompadour that swept over to the right side. Her hair was still parted, but more of her forehead was covered.

She also decided to let her braid down in the back, with a gray ribbon on it to match her eyes. She thought coiling it made her look too old maidish.

"Well, no one could accuse you of being the masculine, window-smashing type of suffragist," E.J. said. "You look very feminine and pretty."

The morning of the ceremony, Rose was a bundle of nerves. Her hands were so cold and trembling she could hardly dress herself. She nearly burst into tears when she popped a button. E.J. quickly sewed it back on, trying to soothe Rose's jangled nerves with reassurance. "You'll do just fine."

Then she went to her bedroom and brought back a wrapped gift.

"It's a little something you might like to take with you today," she said. "Consider it a graduation gift."

Rose tore off the paper and opened the

box. Inside was a beautiful sterling silver mesh handbag. It gleamed with little lights running all through it. It was beautiful, and it suited her dress perfectly.

Then E.J. telephoned for a hack, and they rode to the high school.

Rose took her seat on the stage in the auditorium and looked out over the gathering crowd. She wondered how Mr. Debs did it, getting up in front of a rowdy mob of thousands and thousands of people, speaking as if he were talking to each one of them privately, like a friend.

The exercises began. Rose tried to pay attention to what was going on, but she was too wound up to focus on much other than her own trembling hands, and worrying whether she looked right.

She kept unfolding and refolding the pages of her poems. She looked at the words each time, but forgot them the instant her eyes wandered.

She tried to find E.J. in the audience but couldn't tell one face from another. She was afraid she would simply fly apart before she had a chance to recite her pieces.

A group of junior girls and boys sang the "Boat Song," a round that Rose always found pretty. She sang along, and it helped calm her.

Then Phala Baur got up and gave her oration on Queen Victoria. Vernon Haupt gave a clever, humorous class history that used the name of everyone in the class. He said the Man in the Moon had told him some moonshine secrets and that Sing-Sang, a great Chinese oracle, had given him some historical facts. The Moonman told him that Mr. Schultz had Haupt (hopped) over the Way to Carrie a Rose to Mary only to Phala dozen times, because he was so bashful. It was silly but, Rose thought, very creative.

Then Rose heard her name called out. She stood on wobbly legs, gasping for breath, and walked to the lectern. The pages were limp, and her voice was a little weak at first. But she got her confidence when she heard laughter after the first "They would study, nevermore."

By the third stanza, Rose's nerves had stopped jangling and her voice was clear. At the last line, everyone applauded, long and loud. Then she sat down and let out a big sigh. She was halfway done.

Mary Holt played her piano recital, and the other students gave their presentations.

Then it was Rose's turn to rise again, to give the valedictory speech. Professor Stover introduced her, after a long introduction about Crowley's first high school graduating class.

This time, Rose found her confidence. She so wished she could see the faces of her class-mates, and Professor Stover as she read her speech, but they were sitting behind her.

Mr. Munson and the school board sat in the front row, but Rose chose not to look at them. Instead, she spoke out to the whole audience.

"Homo facit patriam, femina facit domum," she began. The words seemed to roll off her tongue like warm honey. She knew the poem so well by heart that she never once had to look down. She felt confident and pretty

and proud of her accomplishment.

There was polite applause when she sat down. She hadn't expected thundering cries of approval. She knew that most of the audience thought she was simply displaying her learning.

She stole a glance at several of her classmates. Richard Schultz was stifling a laugh. Professor Stover winked at her.

Then there were some songs sung by the younger children, some awards given, and the ceremony was over. Rose floated down the steps of the stage into E.J.'s arms.

"Oh, Rose, I am so, so proud of you. You said you'd do it, and now you have."

Rose hugged E.J. hard and long. She loved her aunt with a fierceness and devotion she had never felt for anyone besides Mama and Papa.

Rose felt a tap on her shoulder. She turned to find the whiskered face of Mr. Munson looking down at her. He was smiling.

"Very good, Miss Wilder. I am glad you saw the wisdom in my remarks. Your poems were both very entertaining. We wish you all the best of luck in your future endeavors."

Rose quickly clapped a hand over her mouth to hide her smirk. Mr. Munson frowned.

"Forgive me," Rose said, trying to calm herself. "It must be my womanly nerves acting up. Thank you."

Mr. Munson shrugged and moved off into the crowd.

Rose turned and looked into E.J.'s eyes. Then they both burst into laughter.

As the crowd swirled around them, Rose realized that in nine short months she had changed and grown more than she had in all the years before. E.J. had shown her the way to become a truly moral person, and a strong woman.

It broke her heart to think that she would be leaving in a few days. She already had her ticket. She dreaded the moment when she must step aboard that train. For an instant, she wondered if she might stay. But she knew she couldn't.

Back in Missouri, Mama, Papa, and

Mansfield awaited her. She missed them all terribly, but she worried what her life would now be like in the little town in the Ozarks. She knew this much: It would never be the way it had been when she left.